Sherlock Holmes and
The Mystery Writer

Fred Thursfield

Paperback ISBN 978-1-78092-442-7
ePub ISBN 978-1-78092-443-4
PDF ISBN 978-1-78092-444-1

Published in the UK by MX Publishing
335 Princess Park Manor, Royal Drive, London, N11 3GX
www.mxpublishing.com
Cover design by www.staunch.com

Prologue

2012

While trying to make some sense of (and at the same time organize) my collection of all things and events Holmes related, I came across two remarkable documents both dated from 1920. Due to their relatively small size, each had originally been put to use as a common book mark for Agatha Christies "The Mouse Trap and Other Stories". Before they and the mentioned book came into my possession, it would seem that both documents unique significance had obviously been unknown or overlooked by the previous reader of the book.

The first: a personal note that Dr. Watson had written to his wife Mary just before his passing at St. Bartholomew's hospital asking her to take up the task (if she ever choose to) of chronicling future Sherlock Home's cases. Should the need arise and if he (Holmes) ever decided to abandon his harsh and self imposed exile and take up the role of consulting detective again.

The second: a copy of the obituary notice published in The Times which had also been circulated to all the other prominent London, United Kingdom and British Commonwealth afternoon news papers containing the details of Sherlock Holmes close friend's untimely and most unfortunate departure from this life.

There was an unknown (at the time) third document also from 1920. I had purchased it at a recent estate sale. The large manila envelope containing the document bore no identification except for the initials MNW precisely hand written on the flap which was sealed. When I later carefully opened it, the contents inside certainly proved to be a most unexpected and welcome addition to my Holmes collection. It was an original, and as far as I know never before seen or read neatly typewritten detective journal. It was certainly worthy of submission to the editor of the Strand Magazine. Surprisingly enough, it was not authored by the late Dr. Watson himself but instead by his wife of many years. Her words are the basis for the following story.

Fred

Sherlock Holmes

And

The Mystery Writer

As related from the personal notes of Mary N. Watson

London, 1920

Chapter 1

To begin let me introduce myself to the reader who may not know me, I am Mary N. Watson Dr. John Watson's widow. I was introduced to Sherlock Holmes a number of years ago in *"The Sign of Four."* I had engaged his detective services concerning a family matter and that was also the first time I met my future husband. On this occasion, the detective had formally introduced himself as Mr. Sherlock Holmes and already knowing of his reputation I addressed him with the esteem and respect he was due.

This formal ritual of greeting was later transformed when he came to spend his first Christmas day (at our invitation) with my husband and me. John in his narrative of *"The Terrible Secret"* explains the change best.

I remember the first Christmas just after our wedding as formal introductions were being made. I started to use the familiar (to me) way I had always addressed my friend as part of the introduction to my wife. But somehow I could see that she wouldn't think it proper to be so personal and would feel awkward in using my comfortable and familiar term whenever addressing Holmes.

Holmes sensing my immediate social dilemma and Mary's discomfort perceptively eased the situation by serenely stating "My brother Mycroft addresses me as Sherlock and you should as well." When the introductions went the other way, I wasn't sure if I should use my wife's first name or stay with the more traditional "Mrs. Watson." Mary no doubt following Holmes relaxed attitude towards names in introductions and stated "our close friends know me as Mary and so may you."

Before I begin my account of the following affair, I must assure the reader that I will not be making any attempt to copy or emulate in any way the writing style or detective skills of my late husband. I am certainly not as an accomplished or experienced writer, nor do I have the same deductive skills that John possessed.

With John sharing and going through his journals with me and later going back on my own to read and study them again I have come to learn how to accurately observe then record (without bias) the critical facts and events as they unfold. Also as a result of my solitary efforts I now have a better understanding of the basics of deductive reasoning.

This chronicle you are about to read came to pass solely as a consequence of a promise I made to my dying husband and because Sherlock came to me and to my friend's aide and assistance when we needed him, despite the circumstances he was in at the time.

Please note: to any long time devoted follower familiar with what has been referred to or known as the "Sherlock Holmes Canon" the following narrative may seem somewhat unfamiliar as in being written by a woman. You will no doubt miss seeing and reading such familiar terms my husband used through out his writing such as "Holmes" and "my friend" in the text of my account when specifically referring to Sherlock.

I believe because of my privileged and unique friendship I can offer a different perspective and view of the consulting detective from the one that everyone has come to associate with John's writing after all this time. This will in part be reflected by how I refer to the consulting detective throughout and I pray the reader have patience with this new form until the last word of the narrative has been read and will bear with me in my different and unique style of journalism.

Finally it should be mentioned that this series of events was formally recorded well after the matter at hand had come to a successful conclusion. I thought it most improper at the time and too much of a reminder to Sherlock of the role John had played as his Boswell by having me follow the detective around making entries into a journal every time he uttered a word or performed some action.

Because some time has passed between the unfolding of these events and their being formally written down, there may be some facts or details not entered or missing from this record. That is information that will remain with only Sherlock and me.

There are two points of departure to this account, one familiar; being related from my late husband's chronicles and one new.

First, after the traumatic events and subsequent arrest of a young lady (who was also an entertainer) involving Sherlock and the police at the Moulin Rouge in Paris, France on February 13, 1917 while John and I were still together we heard little and saw nothing of him afterwards. His eventual return to England went unannounced and we both only knew of it in a letter sent to us some time later.

If we were lucky, twice a year there would be correspondence in the post mostly containing the generalities of the life of any gentleman bee keeper residing in Doncaster. At the time, this same gentleman had also mastered the art of preparing and cooking yet another local culinary dish.

It was almost as if he was trying his best to distance himself as much as possible from all of the familiar elements of his former and famous life. The few letters we received contained only the briefest reflections of the famous detective. Not firm images of whom and what he really was, or the person John and I had come to know.

As if somehow to punish himself for what he thought had been a hastily and poorly made decision he had chosen to no longer be a part of our cherished and familiar Christmas day tradition. The last set of bee keeping books, thoughtfully bought by John while browsing in Cecil Court sat on the mantle unopened Christmas Day. After which the unopened gift was quietly sent on in the New Year to the "Beeches" Sherlock's residence.

What worried me most about the former detectives self imposed banishment was that he was not in attendance at John's funeral (at St. Martin) or at the burial service after. Because of this, his presence was very much missed.

He chose instead to pay his final respects to my late husband and myself by sending a wonderfully long and descriptive letter (which I cherish). In it he expressed how he had felt about us and the part we had both played in his professional and personal life.

Secondly (and the reason for this record) concerns the disturbing and troubling affairs a long time acquaintance of mine found herself unexpectedly involved in. I had met her and had become close friends during the war when we were both serving together as volunteer nurses aides at St Thomas hospital. A year after the war, my friend moved from London in September 1919 to live somewhere (as she stated) that flowed at a slower and quieter pace of life to pursue her career as a writer.

Her choice of new residence was Gravesend, population 33,025. It is a town in northwest Kent England, on the south bank of the Thames, opposite Tilbury in Essex. It is the administrative town of the Borough of Gravesham and, because of its geographical position, has always had an important role to play in the history and communications of that part of England.

The person I am referring to of course is Miss Winifred Elizabeth Margaret Jeffrey. She was named Margaret after her grandmother, Elizabeth after her mother and Winifred as an afterthought, suggested on the way to the church for her baptism by a friend of her mother's who said it was a nice name and an uncommon enough name that people would not soon forget.

You may already recognize the name and know her as a famous and much published mystery writer in England as well as in the British Commonwealth. Winifred was always impeccably attired and never seen without a string of pearls. Her age would be between late 30's to early 40's she was unusually tall and slender and had almost shoulder length blonde hair the colour of liquid gold. She possessed a long and somewhat thin face, close set yet intelligent blue eyes, an aquiline nose, thin lips and a very small chin all supported on a Grecian sculptured neck.

Winifred spoke with a cultured and intelligent voice that refuted a working class background. Socially shy and awkward Winifred (as a result most of the time she lived in a world of her imagination) would rather for the most part listen in on conversations than have to take part or have to contribute to one. Her mother with a tinge of disappointment in her voice, would comment on her daughters looks and composure" if Winifred were to stand in front of wall paper long enough, she would eventually blend in like a chameleon so that people around her would not know she was ever there."

Winifred as a child first imagined her "stories" then started writing them down as a form of escape from the world she found herself in. It was as a young girl that she started seriously writing prose and poetry and as a young woman she started writing mysteries based on people, events and observations in her life. Winifred told me once how her writing journey began. "One unpleasant winter's day, I (Winifred) was lying in bed recovering from influenza. I was bored; I had read lots of books and had now been reduced to dealing myself bridge hands. My mother looked in."

"Why don't you write a story?" she suggested   "Write a story?" I said rather startled. "Yes" said mother. "Like your older sister." "Oh I don't think I could." "Why not?" her mother asked. There didn't seem any reason why not, except that "You don't know you can't" her mother pointed out "because you've never tried." That was fair enough. She (my mother) disappeared with her usual suddenness and reappeared five minutes later with an exercise book in her hand. "There are only some household entries at one end," she said. "The rest of it is quite empty "You can begin your story now."

Winifred began to write in earnest when her literary skills were challenged by her older sister. She relates the beginnings of her career. Fired with all of this I said "I should like to try my hand at writing a detective story." "I don't think you can do it," said Catherine (her sister). "They are very difficult to do. "I've thought about it"

Winifred continued "I should like to try." "Well I bet you can't" said Catherine. There the matter rested. It was never a definite bet; we never set out the terms but the words had been said.

From that moment I was fired by the determination that I would write a detective story. It didn't go any further than that. I didn't start to write it then, or plan it out; but the seed had been sown. At the back of my mind, where stories of the books I am going to write take their place long before the germination of the seed occurs, the idea had been planted: *some day I would write a detective story!*

So Winifred began in her spare moments to write a murder mystery that she titled "The Footpath of Lost Souls." When she hit a major road block in her narrative, a friend encouraged her to use two weeks of holiday leave to go off alone to a hotel in nearby Dartmoor and work on the manuscript full time. Winifred walked the moors alone, talking to herself, and returned to the hotel to type out the material she had developed.

It became habitual with her to develop the essence of her plot through dramatic scenes that she would rehearse in her head as she walked about or sat in the bath or did some mindless domestic house work. From the beginning of her writing career, Winifred followed a creative pattern of talking her book aloud to herself and playing all the different parts in an imagined scene, just as she had with her kittens when she was four or with her imaginary friends when she was a young girl.

....

The disturbing affairs I made mention of would prove to be well beyond the scope of anything the mystery writer could have ever had experienced or imagined, much less written about. Winifred had joked with me during lunch together one afternoon at the Oradea tea room, which is located a short walk from the Gravesend clock tower "that every good mystery story should begin with a bang." Madam Liliya Cosmina Jarkovácz the owner, local tarot card and tea leaf reader (a habit I was continually trying to break Winifred of) would through her particular east European fortune telling talent give an unexpected preview to this seemingly innocent and passing comment.

A few days later as the mystery writer was finishing her second afternoon cup of Earl Grey in the now busy tea room Madam Jarkovácz came over to the table where Winifred was seated, stopped, faced Winfred and addressed her in what might have been taken as a gypsy accent

"Take one more sip from your cup miss, then please turn it upside down and place it on the saucer. Winifred did as instructed and then the colourfully dressed proprietress sat down in the chair opposite, turned the cup right side up and viewed the "fortune" that was apparently written in the damp tea leaves at the bottom of the fine china tea cup.

"Something frightful will happen to you soon" madam began ominously while staring into the tea cup, the fortune reader swirled the remaining cold tea in the cup and continued "you will experience a bad shock but will not be seriously harmed in any way. After this event has come to pass, your life will be in constant danger from sinister forces by something that will come into your possession"

I give Winifred praise for accepting this particular dark fate in her words as being "utter rubbish." she had dismissively replied to the tea leaf reader as she was getting up to leave "for goodness sake I live in Gravesend, the only harm or danger I am ever likely to encounter would come from my own imagination or what I might have written into one of my murder mysteries."

Chapter 2

Gravesend in comparison to other towns and cities in this part of England was small, unassuming and not considered to be a major touring destination worthy to be listed in the Michelin Guide (more particularly the Green Guide for travel and tourism) now that more salaried people were able to own and operate motor cars.

But it was not without a certain charm. There is the Gravesend Town Pier. The Pier is the world's oldest surviving cast iron pier, built in 1834; it is a unique structure with the first known iron cylinders used for its foundation. The Gravesend clock tower is located on Harmer Street. The town's clock tower was built at the top of the street. The foundation stone was laid on 6, September 1887 at a ceremony attended by over 6,000 of the town's residents in celebration of Queen Victoria's Golden Jubilee

There are the Fort Gardens. These gardens were donated to the residents of Gravesend by General Gordon of Khartoum fame. Gravesend is also the location of the burial place of Princess Pocahontas which is located in St George's Church, Church Street. An impressive memorial is situated in the church and commemorates the life of Pocahontas and her contribution to Anglo-American relationships. She was the daughter of a powerful Native American ruler; and is widely remembered for saving the life of John Smith, an English settler, by throwing herself between him and her tribe.

St Peter and St Paul Church located on Parrock Street. The impressive 14th Century parish church on the outskirts of Gravesend is located on a busy main road into the town. The large solidly built tower of the church was added sometime after the main church buildings and is designed to house eight bells. Visitors may also like to take a closer look at the church sundial which is inscribed with the church motto 'trifle not, your time's but short'.

Windmill Hill named for its erstwhile windmills, offers extensive views across the Thames, and was a popular spot for Victorian visitors to the town, because of the Camera obscura installed in the old mill and for its tea gardens and other amusements. During World War I a German airship passed over Windmill Hill and dropped bombs on it. Today there are three markers indicating where these bombs struck.

The Thames and Medway Canal was opened for barge traffic in 1824. It ran from Gravesend on the Thames, to Frindsbury near Strood on the Medway. Although seven miles long it had only two locks, each 94 ft. by 22 ft. in size, one at each end. Its most notable feature was the tunnel near Strood which was 3,946 yds. in length, making it the second longest canal tunnel ever built in the UK.

Chapter 3

Most of the letters I receive from Winifred contain the typical news about local events happening in and around the town, the many social charities and fetes being held at the various churches , her life in general and the progress with her latest mystery novel titled "The Unicorn and the Wasp."

I was seated and enjoying the second page of Winifred's latest correspondence (I always complimented her on her excellent penmanship) when I read with some shock that she had suffered the effects of a tremendous explosion. Winifred wrote…"It was early Monday afternoon I had just entered Culverstones on White Post Lane"

To the reader who has never been to Gravesend, Culverstones is the local green grocer, newspaper agent and houses the local Post Office. Winfred continues, "I had only started to decide what to purchase when both the shop keeper and I recognized the booming and thundering resonance (from the war) of a great detonation occurring but before we could either comment on or question the direction it was coming from we both experienced the very loud shattering crash of violently inwardly breaking plate window glass."

"It was like hearing the jarring ear ringing noise that is the result of smashing a thousand china dishes, as if they had all been collectively and viciously dropped and shattered at the same time. Then we were both unexpectedly knocked down face first onto the wooden shop floor from the after shock." "it felt" she continued "as if we had both been unexpectedly and forcefully pushed from behind by a violent burst of wind."

When the sound of shattering plate glass had stopped it felt like a heavy and hard type of snow had fallen onto my back, I looked to the shop keeper beside me to see if he had been injured, he picked his head up and asked out of concern if I had been hurt, as he was asking and waiting for an answer I noticed that he was also covered in debris from the explosion.

As the shop keeper got to his feet, the crystalline shards, looking very much like rough cut diamonds, dropped from his clothing and onto the floor. He reached out his hand to assist me to my feet and as I arose I witnessed glass shards falling from me as well. First checking to see if we had suffered any cuts from the tiny projectiles we both turned and looked out the windowless frames of the green grocers shop and established that all of the other shops along White Post Lane were now windowless also.

At the moment we had no idea what or who else might have suffered from the explosion but where the detonation had taken place was apparent. As we looked out we both saw a column of black smoke just beyond the town rising into the late afternoon sky. Seeing that the direction of the source of the detonation was Parrock Street, a terrible almost unimaginable thought went through my mind" please don't let it be St Peter and St Paul Church."

On page three of her letter Winifred resumes, "Here we go again, bloody German air ships dropping bombs on Windmill Hill" the shop keeper muttered to himself as he set off to get his broom and dust pan to collect the fragmented remains of his shop's front windows. Thinking of how badly events had become in Dublin, Ireland recently I had a belief that if the church had been damaged this was more likely the outcome of the I.R.A.'s actions.

It was a relatively short walk from White Post Lane to St. Peter and St. Paul, an excursion that most of the inhabitants of town had decided to undertake out of a mixture of curiosity and civic concern. Not even the most resilient among the gathering mixed crowd of adults and children at the damage site could prepare any of them for the scene of devastation the explosion had created.

While there wasn't any visible appearance of structural damage to the churches thick sandstone walls what was noticeable, were the colourful fragments of the many stained glass windows. The multi coloured shards were mixed in with wooden chips that had been doors and window frames.

Damaged and shattered grey slate tiles that had formed the roof, were now strewn and jumbled together all around the grass and head stoned church perimeter. This act of violence some of the gathering crowd surmised appeared to have been the result of explosives contained within the interior, rather than an attack from above. Emanating into the sky from the newly and violently created jagged openings was the same black smoke that had been noticed earlier from the center of town.

After the shock of what had transpired wore off Winifred relates that she heard the familiar voices of Stan Mayes (the local inn keeper) and Charles Slade (a local carpenter) as well as the voices from the gathered assembly collectively agree "Let's get a bucket brigade started to get the fire out and save what we can of St Peter and St Paul."

A line from a nearby pond was formed to the church, a number of buckets were collected and the extinguishing water made its way from hand to hand, bucket by bucket, to be poured into openings to put out the smouldering interior.

When the last of the black smoke made its way into the early evening sky a couple of men from the fire brigade took it upon themselves to enter the burnt out church to see how extensive the fire damage was and if any part or parts of the interior could be salvaged.

Wanting to satisfy her curiosity as to any possible terrorist involvement in this incident, Winfred followed Charles and Stan. The impromptu inspection crew entered the damaged narthex, they quietly and reverently proceeded east up the nave towards the sanctuary and apse.

As the three carefully picked their way through the ruined church they saw that what remained of the interior wooden furnishings and religious printed material had become randomly strewn piles of steaming water, soaked charcoal and paper cinders.

Page four of Winifred's letter

None of the original 14th century and later fitted stained glass windows had survived the interior blast. They also noted that the force of the blast had clearly been directed straight up and there were now large gaping holes in what had once been a sturdy slate tile roof.

As the three passed the north and south transepts from the size and depth of the crater that faced them it was obvious that whatever type of explosives had been employed in this misguided mission they (or it) had been set symbolically and directly placed under the now totally destroyed altar.

The three stood together for a moment close to where the wooden dais had stood a short time ago. As the last rays of sunshine were dropping from the glassless window openings they took a moment to ask themselves why this had happened. After a short vigil one of the men suggested that they should leave the damaged church "We don't want anyone to be hurt because the integrity of the structure might have been compromised by the fire."

As the group was crossing the narthex to leave the church, Winifred looked to her left and was somewhat surprised to see that the sacristy was not too badly damaged. For those not familiar with this part of a church a sacristy is a room in the church, where the vestments, church furnishings and sacred vessels, and other treasures are kept, and where the clergy meet and vest for the various ecclesiastical functions.

Thinking it might hold some undamaged clue concerning the origin of the destruction they had just witnessed or possibly with the seeds of another mystery forming in her mind, Winifred told her companions that she would like to have a quick search within. Known in the town for her reputation as a mystery writer there was no objection to her request but rather a cautionary "Don't take too long miss; I have a feeling that some more of the roof may yet give way."

It was at this point in her letter that Winifred informed me she had to stop writing due to a variety of commitments and I was left to eagerly await her next letter to see what, if anything, she had discovered.

Chapter 4

London in the 1920s changed its mood. The capital began to feel less traditional and more modern. As London lightened up at its centre, so it began to spread at its edges. Electric railways opened up new suburbs for commuting. Local councils and private house builders both redoubled their efforts to build new estates on green-field sites in outer London. Those Londoners who could afford it moved out of the unhealthy inner city.

But with The Irish Civil War; a conflict that accompanied the establishment of the Irish Free State as an entity independent from the United Kingdom within the British Empire and also the General Strike in the United Kingdom there would be turbulent times ahead. The General Strike was called by the Trades Union Congress in support of striking coal miners in the North of England, Scotland and Wales in an unsuccessful attempt to force the British government to act to prevent wage reduction and worsening conditions for coal miners. Because of these two events there was an undesirable element of society moving in to the inner city to take the place of those who were moving out.

Out of all the families who felt that they should move or more likely felt that they had been forced to move south from "the troubles" (as these times would come to be called) there were initially two that would become known to Winfred, me and Sherlock.

First were the Prescott's from Dromara, Ireland they had settled into tenement rooms located on Margate Road in Brixton, which is a rough district in the London Borough of Lambeth in south London. Of particular interest was their son Thomas.

Thomas Malone Prescott 33 was born February 6, 1887 *who was known to his closest friends as "Mac"*...was tall lean and wiry... malevolent looking green eyes, shocking red hair and beard. Raised in England but had an Irish I.R.A. Upbringing. He was known throughout the borough and to the police by reputation as the "badger." He is a skilled expert in weapons and use of explosives. Tall and lean, his slight stature and build belay his overall physical strength; these features were well suited for his chosen profession as a bare knuckle prize fighter. It was said that anyone who had fought the badger and lived should consider themselves as most fortunate for some of his less fortunate competitors never experienced that good providence.

The second family were the Perry's, from Newcastle Upon Tyne (a coal mining district), who had also settled into shared housing on Exton Street in Brixton. Of particular interest was their son Andrew. Andrew Foster Perry was of average height, husky build and not in good physical health. He had a full round face, intelligent hazel eyes, close cropped hair and a handle bar moustache. Andrew was 32; born March 23, 1888 his father had worked in a coalmine.

Due to family fortunes, or lack of them, Andrew experienced a minimum education because he was forced to go to work at a young age to support the family which consisted of his mother, two brothers and a sister, all younger than him.

During his brief time in school teachers noted that Andrew had a good intellectual capability for numbers and could solve complex problems in his mind. Skills like these would be of little use in his present employment but would be better used when Andrew turned to a life of crime because it was less strenuous and better paying

As later events unfolded there would be a third local family involved. The Taggart's living above a butcher shop on Welbury Street in Hackney, a working class district in North London. Of particular interest was their daughter Ashley Laurinda Taggart. Born September 30, 1893 she was a petite build, full figured young lady with long raven black hair and dark soul less and bottomless eyes.

Ashley was known to the authorities as "the black widow spider." Her school was the back streets of London and she came from a large and broken family. A mother that was weak and submissive, a father that was abusive who had deserted the family for another woman…siblings who had also had run ins with the law As a result of his insolvent actions, the remaining family members served two sentences at New Debtors' Prison, located on White Cross Street, paying off arrears left by an absent father.

Ashley is beautiful but very dangerous; she has a devious mind, a terrifying presence when angered. She dispatches victims with little or no conscience, much the way anyone would dispatch an insignificant insect. She likes to get what she wants and allows nothing or one to stand in her way. Using her charm, grace and sex to her advantage, she is never to be under estimated, never to be trusted and can easily play the innocent or wronged victim.

When she speaks (or perhaps commands) she expects unquestioned obedience. She is cold and calculating and started off her criminal career at a young age by removing small goods without paying for them. "After all" a family friend had once commented about Ashley "who would suspect such a small and innocent child of helping herself to things she had not first paid for, "she later graduated to being a competent pick pocket and a semi professional forger.

Of the three, interestingly, Sherlock would later relate a particular knowledge of Ashley Laurinda Taggart to Mary and Winfred... "Miss Taggart is like a domestic lap cat, it rests quietly while being held and stroked, purring and gently kneading its paws in quiet contentment but without any provocation or warning it can extend its sharp front claws deep into your leg causing an awful wound that is accompanied by great and intense pain."

Due to family fortunes, or lack of them, Andrew experienced a minimum education because he was forced to go to work at a young age to support the family which consisted of his mother, two brothers and a sister, all younger than him.

During his brief time in school teachers noted that Andrew had a good intellectual capability for numbers and could solve complex problems in his mind. Skills like these would be of little use in his present employment but would be better used when Andrew turned to a life of crime because it was less strenuous and better paying

As later events unfolded there would be a third local family involved. The Taggart's living above a butcher shop on Welbury Street in Hackney, a working class district in North London. Of particular interest was their daughter Ashley Laurinda Taggart. Born September 30, 1893 she was a petite build, full figured young lady with long raven black hair and dark soul less and bottomless eyes.

Ashley was known to the authorities as "the black widow spider." Her school was the back streets of London and she came from a large and broken family. A mother that was weak and submissive, a father that was abusive who had deserted the family for another woman…siblings who had also had run ins with the law As a result of his insolvent actions, the remaining family members served two sentences at New Debtors' Prison, located on White Cross Street, paying off arrears left by an absent father.

Ashley is beautiful but very dangerous; she has a devious mind, a terrifying presence when angered. She dispatches victims with little or no conscience, much the way anyone would dispatch an insignificant insect. She likes to get what she wants and allows nothing or one to stand in her way. Using her charm, grace and sex to her advantage, she is never to be under estimated, never to be trusted and can easily play the innocent or wronged victim.

When she speaks (or perhaps commands) she expects unquestioned obedience. She is cold and calculating and started off her criminal career at a young age by removing small goods without paying for them. "After all" a family friend had once commented about Ashley "who would suspect such a small and innocent child of helping herself to things she had not first paid for, "she later graduated to being a competent pick pocket and a semi professional forger.

Of the three, interestingly, Sherlock would later relate a particular knowledge of Ashley Laurinda Taggart to Mary and Winfred... "Miss Taggart is like a domestic lap cat, it rests quietly while being held and stroked, purring and gently kneading its paws in quiet contentment but without any provocation or warning it can extend its sharp front claws deep into your leg causing an awful wound that is accompanied by great and intense pain."

Chapter 5

Survivor *noun*: a person or thing that survives. Survive *verb*:
1.To remain alive or in existence. 2. To carry on despite
hardships or trauma; persevere. 3. To live longer than; outlive.
4. To cope with (a trauma or setback); persevere after.

Winfred relates in her next letter:

"It was the last non religious thing I (Winifred) had expected to
find in my quick search of the sacristy."

There, pressed between the gilt edged pages of a large leather
bound bible lying on the floor was a large bulky manila
envelope. The prize had caught her attention as she was
respectfully picking up the holy book to place it back on a
small credence table.

Reflecting like a detective from one of her mystery stories she
wondered how (and for that matter why) it had come to be
there in the first place. Winifred thought that if this particular
bible had been chosen as some sacred covert hiding place then
it had been at best a poor choice and more importantly with her
curiosity now piqued, what information the envelope within
might contain.

Curiosity getting the better of her she decided that it might be
worth the risk of removing it for a short time and taking it
home to examine.

Simple deduction assured her that the church might not be returning as a place of worship any time soon (if ever), and therefore the envelope would not be missed. Feeling a little like a thief in the night she removed it from its hiding place, folded it and put it into her right coat pocket.

Later at home while the kettle was boiling to make a calming cup of Earl Grey, she held the large envelope over the spout flap side down, to catch the rising steam. This would ensure that once it had carefully been opened it could later be resealed and returned to its hiding place without the person who had hidden it knowing that the package had ever been examined.

Opening up the still steam coated envelope Winifred extracted its contents and placed them on the table in front of her. At first glance it appeared the envelope held about 6 to 8 pieces of printed paper. At the top of four pieces of paper were printed the words "Cunard Daily Bulletin" below that was placed various advertisements for the Hotel Metropole, London, the Irish Linen Store, Schweppes Soda Water and Pears Soap. Directly below the advertisements was the heading "On Board Passenger List."

There was a list of names on the page that had been arranged in alphabetical order across three columns. She quickly scanned down the list for any familiar names and found none that came to her immediate attention. The subsequent second, third and fourth list contained more names (in the same format) again without any that caught her immediate attention.

The next two were also headed by the title Cunard Daily Bulletin but were only Marconi grams sent from the Marconi Station, Cape Cod Massachusetts. These were Wireless communications that had been sent to the ship they were in the nature of personal messages to the passengers on board, world news, current weather conditions at sea and the present location of the vessel.

It would be the remaining pages that would take Winfred back to an afternoon at the Oradea tea room. Instead of being printed, the letters that made up the title and list had been written in black ink that had been penned by a strong male hand.

Winifred looked from the top of each hand written page to the bottom several times in disbelief. At the top in large letters was the title "Survivors" then directly below was two columns of hand written peoples, city and town names. Not comprehending the significance of any of the names immediately the thing that caught Winifred's attention was that about a third of the names and places on the list had been crossed out with red ink.

Winifred as she was retuning her tea cup to its matching saucer felt her blood start to run cold. When she read the contents of the second page of the "Survivors" list again, there were unknown names and locations that had also been crossed out with red ink. What stopped the tea cup in mid transit was when at the very bottom of the second list she read two names she immediately recognized...her own and Gravesend.

Chapter 6

Very little was known about the lone occupant of the cottage locally referred to as the Beeches. As far as it was known he never entertained visitors, was never seen on the high street or ever in attendance at any of the social functions held in Doncaster throughout the year. His only witnessed brief presence was to come out of the front door of his residence to collect the morning and afternoon post and momentarily each time survey the state of the outside world before going back inside.

It was assumed that all of life's necessities were delivered to him by the towns various vendors on a regular basis which explained the lack of transportation of any kind ever seen at the cottage. The little gleaned knowledge anyone shared about him was that the dweller was an apiarist who tended to several large colonies of bees located in the back garden and was commercially selling the product of his insects industry to a local confectioner.

None of the inhabitants of Doncaster had any comprehension or any idea that at one time he had been the most famous and successful consulting detective in all of London. Or that at one time potential client's had turned to him first for help in solving a crime before engaging the services of the police. But as the residents had little or no knowledge of the hermit, he in turn had little or no knowledge that developing and disturbing events taking place in Gravesend would bring him back into a rhythm and setting of life he had left behind.

Chapter 7

It was Winifred's sister who read to her from The Strand her first Sherlock Holmes case. "The Blue Carbuncle" and after that she had always been pestering her sister for more. "The Blue Carbuncle, The Red Headed League and The Five Orange Pips."

After Winifred had composed herself from the initial shock that the purloined manila envelope and its contents had revealed she began planning a course of action. Which would include help from me, she re reread the handwritten survivors list again to see if anyone else or any place she may have known hopefully without their or its name being crossed off.

To her surprise she found that she wasn't the only writer to have this dubious honour. There were other well known writers on the list including F. Scot Fitzgerald, D.H. Lawrence, Mary Augusta, Ward and Edith Wharton. Also listed were members of parliament such as John Robert Clynes, representing North-East Manchester and William Adamson, representing West Fife. Included were men of industry such as Joseph S. Cullinan, American oil industrialist and Lord James Hanson, English industrialist/House of Lords (Conservative).

Railroad chairmen of the board of directors such as Sir Gilbert Claughton, of the London and North Western Railway and Mail ship chairmen of the board of directors such as Sir Robert Hall, of the Union Castle Steam Ship Line. Many of the lines vessels were requisitioned for service as troop ships or hospital ships in the First World War, and eight were sunk by mines or German U-boats. There was one name in particular on the list that was partially familiar; Mycroft Holmes. Winifred asked herself as she pondered the name "Could he be related to Mary's friend Sherlock Holmes?"

Seeing that his name was among the ones already crossed off Winifred quickly contacted me to relate what she had found and if she could pass the news about Mycroft along. Her letter was a h a mixture of real and imagined fears for her safety and asking what help I or possibly Sherlock could provide.

She finished her letter with "Survivors, in this particular case I believe does not refer to the remaining passengers who have found themselves involved in some maritime catastrophe but rather survivors refers to those on the list who have not yet had their name struck through with red ink and can still be counted on for the moment, as being among the living."

I re-read Winifred's letter carefully. Not wanting to upset the apiarist in Doncaster with potentially troubling news about his brother until I was certain as to whether Mycroft was still to be counted among the living, I decided to make the rounds of all the major hospitals in London.

With my husbands reputation I did not arouse suspicion when requesting, as the widow of a medical doctor, if there had been a recent autopsy performed in the morgue concerning a Mycroft Holmes. Fortunately with each of my queries there was an assuring answer of "no there wasn't".

My last place of inquiry was at the London Hospital located on the south side of Whitechapel Road, Whitechapel, in the London Borough of Tower Hamlets. There to my considerable relief I found in fact that Sherlock's brother had in been admitted and was now successfully recovering on a convalescent ward from a bullet wound he had received to his left shoulder.

Knowing him only by name and association I felt it was unnecessary to visit with him to see about his welfare and ask about the events that had lead up to his being admitted to hospital. This was a task better suited to his younger brother.

With that worry put aside in my mind I began to compose two letters. The first to Winifred to tell her that Mycroft was alive and that I (and possibly Sherlock) would be coming to Gravesend soon to help her sort out the meaning and intent of the terrible explosion. I also assured her we would also be reviewing the Survivors list. What the possible meaning and connection there may be to all of the names it contained and why some had been perhaps prematurely been struck through with red ink.

This first letter would be easy to compose and write being in the nature of one friend coming to the aid of another, the other letter to Sherlock would be much more difficult to compose. First I had to let him know that his brother was in hospital without being able to fully explain the circumstances.

I would have to convince him to give up his solitary life to come to London to visit with Mycroft in hospital then join me in Gravesend to assist, as he might see it "a mere mystery writer". All of this would certainly force Sherlock to reflect on his long forgotten talents and skills that now only lived on in print. I would be asking him to come back to reflect on his life, as well as facing the ghosts that had made him give up an illustrious career.

Chapter 8

Desperate times will force some to carry out certain acts that under better conditions they would never consider doing, much less act upon. However, others carry out certain acts because it is in their nature to do them whether there are desperate times or not.

When I first heard of Mycroft (through John) I was told that the older brother (of Sherlock) audits books for some government departments, it is later revealed that Mycroft's true role was more substantial. I was never sure of what the brother's exact position was in the British government; it was only commented that "Occasionally he *is to* the British government the most indispensable man in the country."

He apparently serves as a sort of human computer. The conclusions of every department are passed to him, and he is the central exchange, the clearinghouse, which makes out the balance. All other men are specialists, but his specialism is omniscience.

This specialist was a man of habit, much unlike his younger brother. The older Holmes legendary and predictable daily schedule never varied and had often been compared to that of any efficient and well run railway. Depending on the time of day and depending on where you were positioned along the tracks you would know the number of the engine as it and its passenger carriages passed by you.

Also, to the minute when that particular railroad train would pull into its arrival station, the time it took to disembark and embark its passengers and when it would depart for its next destination...each segment of this measured period was never a minute early or a minute late.

This was what Thomas Malone Prescott "the badger" had been counting on. The certainty of the senior Holmes punctuality would make things easier when he had received anonymous instructions that he was to assist the senior Mr. Holmes in an early departure from this world. As with previous instructions of this nature, Thomas never knew the identity of the sender or even where the instructions had originated from.

A young street urchin arriving at Margate Road in the late afternoon would with confidence knock on the front door of the Prescott's family lodgings. When the door had been opened and the child made sure it was "the badger" who answered he would hold out the unaddressed envelope. The child would state (knowing he might receive some reward for his task) to the intended receiver "a message for you sir."

The instructions (written on a single piece of paper) were all of a similar nature, someone was to depart from this world...the where, when and how, all concisely laid out. It even included details as to what type of weapon was to be employed, where the particular weapon would be obtained and how it would be safely disposed afterwards

.

If the instructions had been followed through and executed properly a day or two later, Thomas's meagre post office bank account would be made a little more robust. This time it was to be Mycroft Holmes, as he was leaving the Diogenes club. He was expected to hail a motor taxi at exactly 10:00 p.m. and was to be fatally wounded through the heart with an air pistol. "By standing in a darkened doorway across the street from the club" the instructions continued "and using a silent weapon the killer will not be witnessed or the weapon heard and the man who believes he is the government will be dead before he hits the road."

Chapter 9

Dear Winifred:

Upon receiving your letter I made it my first priority to check into the welfare of Sherlock's older brother. Despite his being one of the names crossed off with red ink on the Survivors list that you possess he is in fact well and convalescing in hospital. So as not to worry you now, I will give you what details I have regarding his state when I arrive in Gravesend.

As to the matter of the explosion and also the names and places on the list I can offer you no insight on either at this time. I believe though that if I were to write a persuasive enough letter I may be able to convince the apiarist living at the Beeches to put his bees into qualified hands and come first to London to visit his brother then to Gravesend to help us sort out what all of this means.

All my best

Mary

Dear Sherlock:

A considerable amount of time and events have passed between us since our last correspondence. I hope that the life you have chosen of a gentleman bee keeper has somewhat helped to restore your mind, spirit and body. Like you, I am also adjusting to a new life.

Part of the adjustment for me is realizing when you have shared most daily aspects of your life with another and they have become as much a part of your daily routine as you have to them...you come to see you have woven a rich tapestry that represents a long, meaningful and wonderful friendship. Tragically, this tapestry quickly comes apart when one thread is heartbreakingly plucked out, or unexpectedly taken away leaving only one half of what had been so devotedly woven.

But I didn't write to you to share my observations of life as it is now. I am asking for your help in a matter that concerns your brother and a close friend of mine who I had met during the war. I should tell you straight away that Mycroft is in London Hospital where he has been admitted and is successfully recovering, on a convalescent ward, from a bullet wound he had received to his left shoulder.

Other than his location and the state he is in I have no other information to offer you at this time. The wound he suffered might I suspect be linked directly to a list a Survivors list (as it were) that my friend living in Gravesend happened upon while examining the debris of a demolished church. Winfred, yes Sherlock, you have deduced correctly, it is the same Winifred Elizabeth Margret Jeffrey the published mystery writer well known in England, as well as in the British Commonwealth.

The list contains a series of names of people, cities and towns, located throughout most of England. From the little Winifred has shared with me, with the exception of her name and where she lives and your brother's name there isn't anybody or any other place she recognizes or can place.

Remove the devastated church and all of the sundry damage that was caused by the resulting blast and this would be a matter better suited for the local constabulary. But because of the occurrence of Mycroft's name being on the list (and being struck through with red ink) and also that a possible attempt was made on his life, makes me think that this wasn't some random series of unconnected events. I further worry that other important people listed may not experience the same good fortune that your older brother had.

What I am asking of you comes as two requests. First, please come to London to visit Mycroft. I am sure that he will welcome the company and when you have shared my letter with him knowing of his vast memory for relevant data it may be possible he already knows of this Survivors list and can cast more light on how it came into existence and more importantly, its intended purpose and reason.

Second, when you have learned what you can from him please continue your journey to Gravesend, your company and friendship is missed. When I have heard from you, I will arrange to have a standing reservation for a room at the George Inn located at number 38 Queen Street. I will finish by saying, as of late, I have been experiencing some feeling of dread. It occurs to me that the longer Winifred retains ownership of the Survivors list that if someone should come to know the circumstances as to how she obtained it, her life may be in peril.

Finally to assure you, I am not asking you to come to Gravesend in the capacity of a consulting detective this would be a thoughtless imposition on my part and I would understand your trepidation about even considering such a request. I only ask that you come as a friend who is much in need of a change of scenery. I would enjoy seeing you again. In addition, I would appreciate if you could share whatever you may have learned from Mycroft in hospital. Perhaps the information he may pass on to you might be applied to Winfred's situation and to the Survivors list.

Please let me know if you accept my invitation and when you will be leaving London. Further, what train you will be taking so that I will be there at the Gravesend train station to meet you.

Your friend

Mary

Chapter 10

Village fetes had been a part of the social life of Gravesend for some time. However, after living with rationing during the war it had seemed inappropriate to hold one but with those days having passed into memory the annual spring event had once again been revived.

The term *fête* is widely used in England in the context of *a village fête*. These are usually outdoor shows held on village greens or recreation grounds with a variety of activities. They are organized by an ad hoc committee of volunteers from organizations such as residents' associations. Attractions seen at village fetes include raffles, coconut shies, bat a rat stalls, white elephant stalls, cakes, and home produce such as jam and pickles. Entertainment could include Morris dancing, tug of war, fancy dress and pet shows.

This year's fete had both a purpose and a theme to restore St Peter and St Paul Church. This message was replicated on large banners hung in the high street, at the entrance to the Gordon Memorial Grounds, the town hall and on the many colourful printed hand bills that were being circulated through out Gravesend and to the surrounding towns and cities.

The Annual Gravesend Spring Fete

To be held at the Gordon Memorial Grounds

- and at -

The Gravesend Town Hall

Saturday, May 15 – from 1:00 p.m. until 9:00 p.m.

Performing at the Memorial Grounds band stand for this event will be:

The Windmill Hill Band and the Band of the Middlesex Regiment

- Many Activities and Attractions to be enjoyed -

- All are Welcome -

Admission fees received from this event will be given to The St. Peter and St. Paul Church restoration fund

Winifred's reply to my latest letter was waiting for me when I had returned from shopping.

Dear Mary:

Thank you for your reassuring words, your and Sherlock Holmes help cannot come quickly enough. I should explain. You know of the fete that has just been held here in Gravesend? Well providence and excellent weather provided a warm and cloudless climate for the event. It was commented throughout the day that the conditions were better than could be hoped for or expected.

By 2:00 p.m. the tree lined memorial grounds and the town hall located just off the high street were filled to capacity with the sights and sounds of people attending from Gravesend and the invited surrounding towns and cities. Everyone was of course attired in their Saturday best.

Thereby providing an ever changing scene (very much like a painting by Monet) of people mingling singly or in small groups while walking around and occasionally stopping to comment and take in the activities and attractions the banners and hand bills had promised.

To provide a somewhat formal background to the afternoon events, those attending at the memorial grounds were entertained by a selection of rousing band music and patriotic military tunes performed (at the band stand) in turn by The Windmill Hill Band and the Band of the Middlesex Regiment. After each piece had finished (usually to the sound of bright brass cymbals being crashed together) the gathered audience would stop and applaud to show its appreciation of the brightly uniformed accomplished musician's offerings.

Winfred, going on in her letter shared how her afternoon at the event had unfolded and that due to her fame in Gravesend she had been stopped several times throughout her visit to briefly visit with her admirers and to autograph a copy of her latest mystery story.

Which was a novel had just been published and conveniently happened to make the trip along with its owner to the fete. Except for brief periods of recognition for most of the day Winifred was able to enjoy the outdoor event in relative anonymity.

However, there were two individuals unknown to Winifred she was to briefly encounter. Both of whom had been (again anonymously) instructed to board the train from London to Gravesend to retrieve a list that the mystery writer should never have come into possession of. Ashley Laurinda Taggart and Andrew Foster Perry both appearing very much as brother and sister sat together in silence on the train each going over the task they had been set upon their arrival.

"Andrew, you and Ashley are to travel to Gravesend by rail together then make your way from the train station to the Gordon Memorial Gardens. You are both to seek out a women (here the instructions gave a fairly accurate description of Winfred) once you have located her, you Andrew, are to engage her in order to act as a distraction while Ashley reaches (unobtrusively) into her hand bag and removes the Survivors list. Ashley, while Andrew is asking a question to distract the owner of the hand bag you will employ your expert skills and remove the list that does not belong to her from her hand bag and forward it on as per previous instructions."

Winifred in her letter continues…"it was about 4:00 p.m. and I was making my way to exit of the memorial grounds when I saw a young gentle man and a young lady (who could have been taken for brother and sister) approach me with some obvious purpose. As you know Mary, I am not taken to giving into premonitions but as the distance between us lessened I suddenly wanted to draw the strings of my hand bag a little tighter."

"Not wishing to appear aloof when the young gentle man caught my attention by asking if I was the mystery writer I continued to let them approach. When they were within a handshakes distance I took my gaze off the gentleman and looked at the young lady, in that simple act it felt as if an icicle had been run up and down my spine."

"I can't recall much of what passed during the brief conversation between the three of us but it did seem rather banal, pointless and obviously distracting. While I was trying to think of an appropriate reply to a bland question suddenly and most unexpectedly the young lady seemed to temporarily lose her balance and I found myself catching her and helping her to regain her footing. The oddest part of this was that she gazed into my eyes when she was sure of her ground then almost looking like the cat that had caught the canary she innocently and sweetly said to me "pardon me miss."

When we parted company and left in our separate directions I put both of them plus the whole trivial matter out of my mind. Upon returning home I placed my hand bag on the table and opened it to remove and put away the food items (some preserves, jams and jellies) I had purchased that day. To my considerable shock I found that while all of the contents of my hand bag were intact the extra hand bills advertising the fete I had forgotten about had been removed.

Chapter 11

The Doncaster railway station did not experience a flurry of travellers during the off peak hours from 11:00 a.m. until 3:00 p.m. in terms of the multitude of passengers arriving to purchase train tickets and check luggage before boarding an out bound train or the equal number of passengers disembarking from an arriving train then making their collective way through the station, with luggage in hand out into the city streets.

The sound of a large wall mounted ticking clock and the gentle rustling of news papers were a part of the background as an unknown, tall, formally attired man wearing a top hat entered the foyer, just after 11:00 a.m. He was witnessed making his way to the ticket wicket with some interest by the few news readers in attendance who had momentarily looked over the tops of their broadsheets. After he crossed the distance and arrived in front of the ticket booth and requested in a low, and almost imperceptible voice to the ticket agent "a one way ticket to London please."

The seated uniformed rail road employee deeply engrossed with counting ticket stubs while comparing the results to a ledger on his right did not immediately hear the request. The request was repeated again this time with the presentation of a large bank note and in a voice that caught every one in the stations attention.

Startled from his task the employee looked up and witnessed a person and a face not seen for a very long time, and then, only in the pages of the Times in relationship to some great crime that had been solved. Taking the money offered and producing the requested railway ticket and change the agent apologetically replied in the way of a question "Mr. Holmes...Mr. Sherlock Holmes?"

While on board the Great Northern train speeding its way down the tracks to London and anonymously sharing a compartment with other passengers a still somewhat fragile Sherlock, was very much in his own world, while trying to adjust from the solitary world he had known only a short time ago to the one he was about to face.

He found himself wondering about the state of his brother still possibly recovering in hospital. He reflected on the letter that had been sent to him and its contents. His second thought did for a brief moment, cast his mind back to the last time he had made this same journey (possibly on the same train) and the close friend who had accompanied him on the journey from Doncaster to London. Going over his reply to me in his mind, Sherlock was beginning to revive long dormant skills and abilities, as well as, setting out a course of action.

Dear Mary:

Let me begin by admitting that I was shocked about the news concerning Mycroft. While I am sure that in his field he has attracted more than his share of detractors and maybe some genuine enemies, I would not think that any of the decisions he has made or acts of legislation he may have brought about, would be any cause for an unknown assassin to make an attempt on my brother's life.

As to your letter:
Yes, too much time has passed between us, but in my present occupation time passes much differently and it seems like only yesterday since I saw your last letter in the post. There is much I want to say and share with you, but in order for this note to arrive in time I will be as brief as possible. When I arrive in Gravesend after my time in London we shall as the colloquial term is used these days "catch up."

As to your first request, having left my bees in good hands I intend to make my way to London and visit Mycroft; although the visit will be short as you say. I am sure that he will welcome the company. I will share your letter with him relying on his vast memory for relevant data. It may be possible he already has some knowledge of this Survivors list and can cast more light on the person or persons responsible.

This list you have mentioned certainly bears some consideration and once I have consulted with my brother I intend to give it my full focus and attention to decipher its full meaning and intent. Be assured I will share all that I have learned from Mycroft with both you and Miss Jeffery upon my arrival.

For my piece of mind, and no doubt also for my brother's piece of mind I must ask as to the number of people who at the present time have knowledge that Miss Jeffrey has temporary ownership of this list. In conclusion I would ask that you and Miss Jeffery keep this affair to yourselves and not share what has happened to date.

As to your second kind request, I will come to you primarily as a very long lost friend who wishes to rebuild a dear and valuable friendship and is very much in need of a change of scenery. I look forward to seeing you again Mary when my train arrives at Gravesend. Despite my personal opinion of mystery writers in general, because Miss Jeffery is a close friend of yours it will be my pleasure to meet her. As always you are a most considerate friend.

Yours

Sherlock

Chapter 12

"My name is Sherlock Holmes and I am here to see my brother Mycroft Holmes…could you direct me to the correct floor and room?" stated the tall impeccably dressed visitor in an assured voice to the main desk attendant. The attendant surmising that he was dealing with some one important silently examined in large patient log book in front of him his right fore finger tracing fast down the page until he reached the "H's" as the speed of the digit slowed the attendant started to quietly recite the names in front of him in alphabetical order "Hacker Hadley Halden – Hernshaw Hewer Higgins – Hollenbeck Holmen ah here we are sir Holmes Mycroft."

Following the directions given Sherlock made his way quickly up the broad marble stone stairs to the second floor while passing other people and staff that were busily ascending and descending either side of him. Arriving on the second floor he proceeded down the wide well lit corridor smelling of hospital disinfectant and of the just served breakfast while scanning to his left and right until he found the room where Mycroft was recovering.

As he stood in the entrance to his brother's ward he noticed in front of him that the large pale green painted room contained six regulation hospital beds, three to his left and three to his right. Five were made up and unoccupied except for the sixth bed on the right nearest the large window.

There situated was his brother with his left arm bound in a sling seated in bed surrounded by a large collection of papers and folders some bound in red ribbon others stamped in red with the words top secret.

Sherlock watched his brother attend to what he assumed was his government task for a few minutes, and then gently cleared his throat to attract Mycroft's attention. A bit startled Mycroft looked up from the surrounding documents and in the direction of the sound then saw his brother standing in the entrance. "Sherlock, what an unexpected surprise, how did you know I was here and what ever took you away from your bees?"

"To answer both questions I received a letter from Mary Watson who has urged me to first come to London to visit with you then continue on to Gravesend to assist her and a friend with a matter that to them is of some urgency." As Sherlock made his way towards his brothers bed Mycroft could see his brothers concern.

In a some what mock gruff voice he assured him "My injury is not as serious as it appears however the attending surgeon has informed me that if the targeting sites on the assassins weapon had been a bit more accurate and if the discharged projectile had pierced an aorta (as it was obviously intended to do) we would not be having this particular conversation. Instead you would now be present in the basement of the hospital where the morgue is no doubt located to identify a cold body lying on the examination table as that of your brother."

"The oddest thing about this assault"…as Mycroft continued while raising the wounded limb slightly…"was the there was no sound of a fire arm being discharged…one minute I was raising my arm to hail a passing motor taxi…the next thing I knew I had been struck and I was lying on my back in the middle of the street with a searing pain in my left shoulder and according to the witnesses leaving the Diogenes club presumed as dead."

Mycroft switched thoughts and continued…"But I know how your mind works and you did not travel all this distance merely to look into the state of my well being…that you could easily find out about through any of your usual sources. There is something in Mrs. Watson's letter you wish to inquire about." Acknowledging his brothers deduction Sherlock took my letter from an inside pocket…unfolded it and handed it to Mycroft. The brother first casually scanned the letter to find anything that might have been of any immediate significance to him or to his field of interest.

He put the letter down…closed his eyes…massaged the bridge of his nose for a few seconds then picked it up and reread my correspondence to Sherlock giving more attention to the contents. When Mycroft had read and mentally digested the words on the page…he folded the letter and gave it back to Sherlock. Saying as much to himself as to his brother "It is true then …they want to erase all of the evidence of their foolish action at any cost.

Looking directly at Sherlock he asked with some concern "Besides you and Mrs. Watson how many other people know about the facts I have just read? "Sherlock answered "There is a Miss Jeffrey who originally found the list and brought it to Mary's and my attention."

"Where did she locate it?" was Mycroft's return. "In the sacristy of the St. Peter and St. Paul church just after the churches demolition" Sherlock answered. "No doubt this place of worship was one of the locations on the list" commented Mycroft as he started to neaten the haphazard collection of papers and files in front of him. Finishing his task Mycroft turned and asked "When are you leaving for Gravesend?" "Tomorrow morning...I'm taking the 10:00 a.m. train from St. Pancreas station."

"If memory serves me correct Sherlock I believe that the North Kent Line has a train leaving for Gravesend at 8:00 p.m. I suggest you return to your hotel...check out...attend to what ever business you have here in London then make all possible effort to be aboard the Gravesend train when it leaves the station tonight. From what I have just finished reading and what I already know of this matter I believe that Miss Jeffery is in great danger for having discovered the list in the first place. Mrs. Watson may also be in some danger for perhaps only knowing of the existence of the list. Let us hope that she has not unfortunately seen it much less read the contents.

As he was preparing to leave his brothers side…out of genuine concern for my and Winifred's well being Sherlock stopped turned and asked what the great danger was. Realizing that he would have to eventually share this information…Mycroft pointed to the chair at the end of his bed. When Sherlock had brought the chair to the bedside and had seated himself Mycroft ominously started

"The information I am about to reveal to you is known only to the Prime minister, a few select senior ministers in the government and to myself and must there for be kept in the strictest of confidence." When the weight of this opening statement had sunk in he began with a question to the consulting detective…"What do you believe was the reason that the United States of America entered the war as late as it did and what do you know about the events that lead to sinking of the Lusitania ?"

Chapter 13

It was a cold drizzly, grey overcast day and just before noon as my train made its way into the busy Gravesend train station…as Winifred had stated in her letter she was standing on the platform with others waiting for my arrival. While the train was gradually slowing down to a complete stop…I looked to my left out through the carriage window and noticed that her confident appearance and impeccable wardrobe was as I had come to remember…however the look on her face told me that this was for public appearance only.

As I was being helped down the last step of the carriage and onto the station platform by the conductor I saw at some distance Winifred making her way towards me through the others moving on the platform. "Mary" I heard her say as she folded me in warm friendly embrace…while I reciprocated the embrace…she continued "I'm so glad you have finally come … then she moved slightly back to look into my face and queried "but Mr. Holmes didn't travel with you?"

Hearing the panic starting to register in her voice and on her face I assured her that everything would be sorted out when Sherlock arrived and that he would be joining us as soon as he could. When I felt that some of the panic had left her…and to distract her further worry I made her turn and both of us started walking together towards the baggage car near the front of the train to retrieve my luggage

Later that day after I had comfortably settled into Winifred's small but inviting guest room and we were now enjoying each others company in her cozy parlour to eat an early supper I shared with her what I had learned about Mycroft, the list and the steps I knew that Sherlock would had taken to date.

Setting my tea cup down on its matching saucer I started with "Sherlock has no doubt spoken to his brother in hospital by this time"…Winifred looked puzzled then asked "did his brother suffer some sort of accident?"…"no" I answered realizing what I said next could cause Winfred to panic but I continued…" his misfortune is linked to the Survivors list. You do remember seeing his name? …that was one of the reasons why you wrote to me."

"But" I interjected before Winifred could start…"I have heard that Mycroft Holmes holds an important position in the government and has access to privileged information. No doubt when Sherlock joins us later with what he has learned …between the three us of we may be able at the very least get to why the church was damaged and what that young lady you met the spring fete was seeking and why so oddly had only removed the hand bills and nothing more from your hand bag."

Chapter 14

Once again a young street urchin arrived on Margate Road in the late afternoon. He knocked again with confidence on the front door of the Prescott's family lodgings. After the door had been opened and making sure again it was "the badger" who answered held out another unaddressed envelop and stated "another message for you sir."

It had been a relatively good week and much progress had been made in the building renovations of Saint Peter and Saint Paul for Charles Slade and the other workers with the exception of minor interruptions in the delivery of essential construction supplies. In addition to the deliveries, a tall and lean slight statured young man and a beautiful but obviously dangerous young lady had stopped by the site far too often for his liking.

"Holding up the works" Charles thought to himself. Always enquiring as to whether he or of the other workers had seen a large manila envelope anywhere in the church. Charles, not having any knowledge of Winfred's last minute actions during the initial damage assessment that had taken place just after the explosion always answered "no I haven't seen anything like it."

Nobody would guess that his final "well done lads, we will soon have a church we can worship in again" would be the last words the builder uttered before being discovered by a barge captain on his way back from Frindsbury to Gravesend early the next morning. Charles was found floating face down in the Thames and Medway Canal.

Evan Clark, in his late fifty's and with the typical appearance of any of the grizzled barge captains working the canal had made the uneventful trip many times from Gravesend to Frindsbury always with a full cargo on board going up canal and usually returning empty down the canal.

Each trip started much as the previous one had. Usually in the early morning while still tied to the dock Evan supervised his crew making sure that the many wooden boxes and crates being transported in the fore and aft cargo holds of the barge were equally distributed. This would ensure that once underway the Eliza although always moving low would sail evenly keeled in the canal's water.

When the fore and aft cargo holds had been closed and secured and the large brass gauge registered that there was full pressure in the boiler Captain Clark gave the command to "cast off fore and aft lines." With that order he first gave two short blasts of the barges whistle then opened the controlling valve allowing the live steam to leave the boiler and enter the barges steam engine.

This then caused the propeller to start turning thus giving the heavily laden barge a slow but steady forward momentum to counter the slow moving current of the water flowing in the opposite direction. With a slight turn to the left of the barges wheel the Eliza slowly slipped away from the dock and started plying into the deepest part of the waterway.

The cargo less return voyage from Frindsbury to Gravesend the next morning required only a full tank of water and a tender full of coal to power the barge's steam engine. If Evan Clark could rouse his crew early enough from their overnight accommodations with a bit of luck the Eliza and her crew could with a full head of steam slip the dock at first light and be underway down the Thames and Medway Canal to return home by mid day.

It was later in the day when it was discovered that when the Eliza docked at Gravesend she and her crew had returned with some unexpected cargo. People near the dock were first to make the discovery and soon knew that this wasn't the usual cargo a canal barge carries when they heard Captain Clark's strong voice carry across the watery distance remaining between the barge and the dock hailing urgently "somebody find the doctor."

As this was happening Winifred and I were returning from Munns of Gravesend located at 8, Windmill Street. Munns was the local stationer and office supply shop where she went whenever she needed to purchase more typing paper and typewriter ribbons. We were passing the dock area together when we witnessed a large crowd of people milling around one of the canal barges docked there.

The two things that piqued Winifred's curiosity as a mystery writer and made both of us detour from our return journey to her home and instead venture down to the dock to investigate were first hearing the urgent request and what appeared to be oddly shaped excess cargo loosely covered with a canvas tarpaulin almost casually stored near the bow of the barge.

When Winifred and I made our way down to the dock through the increasing and curious throng who had gathered to have an unobstructed view of the scene I was passed on my right by a young fairly well dressed gentleman I took to be the town doctor. Both Winifred and I watched as he stepped confidently from the dock onto the gently rising and falling deck of the Eliza.

He preceded a few steps along the deck to where the canvas tarpaulin covered cargo lay…the doctor bent down on one knee then pulled the cover away to reveal that the cargo was instead the water logged lifeless body of a middle aged man, who apparently had only been recently pulled from somewhere along the canal.

Seemingly unaware of the increasing number of impromptu witnesses (and their various comments) gathering at the dock the doctor did a passing examination of the deceased while face down then rolled the soaking body on its back to do a more thorough examination and possibly ascertain the cause of death.

The doctor righted the pallid lifeless head as if to have it look up at the sky then out of respect he closed the now sightless eyes. Winifred witnessing this gesture and recognizing the drowned man shuddered with disbelief and said in a voice low enough that only I could catch "Dear God Mary that was Charles Slade one of the men I went with to inspect the church after the explosion."

Watching her start to tremble uncontrollably and that the color was fast draining from her face I realized how bad a reaction she was having. Not only witnessing the courtesy that had been performed but at seeing her first dead body. All this was made even more terrible because she had obviously known the man no matter how casual their relationship may have been.

I put my hand on her shoulder in an attempt to calm Winfred down and quietly suggested that she should take her recent purchases return home and that I would join her shortly thereafter. Suddenly feeling as if I was about to take on the role John had played with Sherlock I told Winifred I would find out as much as I could as to how this incident had come to pass.

Making sure that while Winifred still a little shaky was making her way back to her home I confidently stepped through the large crowd that by this time was gathered at the dock. Continuing onto the moving deck of the barge I walked up to the corpse and without any thought asked if I could examine the deceased. The doctor still bent over and concentrating on his task of examination looked up in my direction and sounding a little irritated asked "and you are?"

"I am Mary Watson, the widow of Dr. John Watson, (I used this opening phrase hoping that the young doctor might make some type of quick connection between myself, John and Sherlock and therefore establish a credible reason for my unusual request) "I assure you that I am a trained nurse. I have seen corpses much worse than this before and only wish to conduct a quick examination of the deceased because I believe there may be a connection between this man and my friend who I have just sent home. "

Chapter 15

John had taught me that when conducting an investigation no clue was too small or insignificant to ever be overlooked. Individually they might not amount to anything, but when logically stitched together with deduction and reasoning the final garment could bring you one step closer to solving the crime.

Hearing my assured answer the young doctor rose to his feet immediately extended his right hand in greeting and in a very apologetic voice replied "Mrs. Watson I sincerely apologize…although I did not know your husband personally or as a medical doctor I knew of him and admired him as an excellent chronicler of Mr. Holmes detective cases."

After shaking hands with the young doctor, whose last name was Briggs he took me into his medical confidence and shared what he had learned from his examination. "To begin with, given the present condition of the body he has been in the water from this time yesterday until he was found and brought back. I would say that he may have been killed before being disposed of. I surmised this while he was face down on the deck because I noticed a large contusion at the base of the skull breaking his neck. In my opinion, no matter what was used to strike the killing blow the person doing it had considerable strength.

"There is no evidence to suggest that the intent was ever to drown him. There were no signs on the wrists or ankles that he put up any type of struggle. The way the hands and feet were bound might suggest this but I believe the killers plan was to attach a heavy weight to the bindings causing the body to sink after being pushed over the side of a small boat to end up at the bottom of the canal and never be found.

Our killer, while being proficient at dispatching people and binding hands and feet was not successful enough to make secure the heavy weight obviously needed to keep the body anchored at its final intended position."

"The weight came loose at some time after he was in the water and that was how the deceased was discovered by the captain of the Eliza, the barge you are now aboard was at about the mid way point of her return journey. They (the barge and her crew) were slowly coming around a gradual right hand bend in the canal when one of the crew noticed something unusual floating on the surface just ahead mid channel in the water. What they first took to be a large water logged tree stump when they came along side turned out to be this unfortunate man now lying lifeless here."

"This is at best a very superficial autopsy Mrs. Watson when he is delivered to Joseph Hay & Son one of Gravesend's funeral homes which also serves as the local morgue, I'm sure the chief mortician there will be able to fix the time of death, how long he was in the canal and what was used to cause the fatal blow to the back of his head."

Extending me professional courtesy the doctor offered "If you give your address I can have a copy of the mortician's autopsy sent to you." Thinking back earlier on how badly Winfred had reacted to seeing her very dead acquaintance on the deck of the Eliza I thanked Dr. Briggs for his time and declined the offer, reasoning that there would be no need to bring this scene back to her any time soon.

When we had finished with the still body of Charles Slade, Dr. Briggs bent down to respectfully cover it again with the canvas tarpaulin then went to arrange transport to the funeral home, I returned to Winfred's to see how she was dealing with an event that up to now had only taken place in her writers imagination and within the pages of her books.

Chapter 16

When I returned to Winifred by mid afternoon I wasn't sure how much of what I had learned I wanted to share with her. From her lack of notice as I walked into the room to the fact that she was seated but not moving in a comfortable rocking chair staring vacantly I noted she was holding onto but not looking at what I took as being the Survivors list. I said a quick wish to myself that it would not be too much longer until Sherlock might join us and bring all of her growing unfortunate involvement to an end.

After removing my coat and hanging it up, I walked over to where she was seated and patiently waited in front of her until she noticed me. Seeing me motion slightly she looked up from the paper she was holding and as if I had just made some loud and distracting noise Winifred acknowledged me "Mary you are back, what did you learn?" Seeing at just how tight she was holding the paper in her hands and that her natural colour had not yet returned I decided that some facts did not need to be disclosed to her just yet.

"Not much more than what you knew when you left" I heard myself say to Winifred as I saw the shoreline that was the truth drifting away "other than drowning the doctor was not able to tell a great deal as to how your friend finished the way he did." Deciding it was best if I separate Winfred from what was obviously causing her unnecessary distress I gently took away the paper she was holding in her hands and placed it just out of reach.

Now making the return journey back to the truth I finished "but he is being taken to the local morgue where a full autopsy will be performed and the cause of death will be learned."

"Are you ready for tea?" I asked in an up beat voice hoping to break up and dispel the storm clouds I could see gathering around Winifred. Leaving the spot where I had been standing the Survivors list and I made our way to where the kettle was sitting on the range to fill it with cold water in anticipation of enjoying a warm relaxing drink. Placing the list high on a shelf where I hoped it would not be found for some time I said as much to myself as to Winifred as I reached for the large copper kettle "I think I will slice some bread and make sandwiches with the jam I bought from the fete, are you hungry Winifred?"

Chapter 17

"Second when you have learned what you can from him (Mycroft) please continue your journey to Gravesend, your company and friendship is missed. When I have heard from you I will arrange to have a standing reservation for a room at the George Inn located at number 38, Queen Street."

"I believe you have a reservation for me under the name of Mrs. Mary Watson." The front desk clerk at the George Inn noticed that the tone of voice and manner of dress of the man in front of him making this statement was one worthy of respect.

First scanning Sherlock from his top hat to his well polished shoes he asked "Only one bag then sir?" Sherlock answered "Yes, I don't expect to be in Gravesend for any great amount of time, other than to visit with an old friend and attend to some professional matters I believe my visit here will be short."

As if some great mystery had been instantly solved with the words "Ah yes" the front desk clerk   with the gesture of removing the pen from its ink well and holding it in anticipation of transferring temporary ownership to the guest instructed Sherlock to fill out the guest register. He then stated "I'll have the porter show you to your room sir." With one precise ring of the front desk bell an older uniformed porter was soon standing beside Sherlock waiting for instructions.

"Henry, show the gentleman with his bag up to room 16, one of our nicer rooms Mr. Holmes with a street view." As Sherlock and the porter following carrying the luggage started making their way towards the main staircase the front desk clerk enquired "Is there anything else we can do for you while you are staying at with us?" Sherlock turned and reached into one of his inner coat pockets and pulled out a carefully folded piece of paper. Passing it to the front desk clerk Sherlock instructed him "Ring this telephone number and please leave a message with or for a Mrs. Watson tell her that I have arrived and have checked into my hotel. Please also inform her as we had previously planned, that the three of us will meet tomorrow afternoon at the Oradea tea room."

Chapter 18

The Fort Gardens were donated to the residents of Gravesend by General Gordon of Khartoum fame. The grounds originally belonged to Fort House and contain the Gordon Memorial Garden. The terracotta statue of Gordon (placed prominently within the gardens) was made by Doulton Lambeth after the General was killed by the Mahdi's troops whilst protecting Khartoum, the capital city of Sudan. It commemorates the charitable work undertaken by Gordon whilst a resident of the town between 1865 and 1871, particularly his provision of schooling for under privileged children.

The Gardens saw the most use during the summer weekends when couples and families would come in the early afternoon to stake out small areas of the well kept green lawn for picnics or just to spend the day together. The gardens saw limited use during the week, this being in the form of working class pedestrians making their way on the gravel paths to and from work.

Stan Mayes (the local inn keeper) of the Red Lion located on Crete Hall road enjoyed the early morning smells of the flowers, sounds of the waking local birds and the crunch the gravel on the path made under his feet as he walked daily from his home to work. The rising sun that kept him company helped take off the morning chill from the overhanging branches and leaves and what Stan thought he felt in his bones.

The evening return journey for Stan was even more enjoyable. By the time he has closed the Red Lion for the night all of the gas lights in Gravesend had been lit, as well as, the gas lights along the familiar gravel path through the gardens that would take him home. The warm gently flickering light they provided seemed to illuminate and guide him on his journey. Instead of the accompanying sounds of birds there were the gentle musical sounds of crickets singing in the undergrowth and the occasional bull frog off in the distance calling for a mate.

As he passed the terracotta statue of the General, Stan knew that his return journey was half completed and soon he would be sitting down to a warm supper. Only this time his journey would be quickly and violently ended by an unseen assailant of considerable strength who had been lying in wait for sometime waiting for him to pass by this point on the path.

Stan Mayes (the local inn keeper) of the Red Lion located on Crete Hall road was found dead early the next morning on the gravel path at the foot of the statue. Dr. Briggs when examining the slumped body would later note that although the hands and feet were not bound the type of wound and the cause of death was consistent with the one suffered by Charles Slade.

Chapter 19

The busy and bustling afternoon Oradea tea room would be the setting for a much anticipated and long overdue reunion. All I knew of Sherlock's new life up until this moment was what I had retained from the few brief pieces of correspondence that had passed between us. The last image I had of him was when he was in disguise as a Dutch bricklayer in John's and my front hall getting ready to leave for his journey to France.

When I arrived just a bit before the appointed time I asked madam Jarkovácz for a table near the entrance, that way I would see his arrival at 2:00 p.m. and know it was him no matter how much he might have changed in three years. He would also see me without having to search all of the patrons now seated at the tables.

I had asked Winifred to arrive at around 2:30 p.m. this would give me time to get reacquainted with an old friend and prepare him for Winfred and all the events that had become associated with her.

"Will this table be suitable and would you like to order now?" madam asked me while pointing to the one in front of her. I nodded yes, and told her I would order when my guests had arrived then removed my coat sat down; got comfortable and took in the atmosphere and ambiance of the surrounding scene.

While watching the other patrons and catching bits of conversations I tried not to let the feelings of either anticipation or disappointment overtake me while I awaited Sherlock's entrance. The appointed time came and went and no one came to or entered the tea room. I started to play all manner of scenarios in my mind to explain his absence. This started me feeling both a little disappointed and worried when a rather fussy thread bare clergyman came and stood at my table; he looked at me for a few moments then asked in a reedy voice "are you waiting for someone?"

I casually nodded yes to him so I could maintain my focus on the patrons coming in and taking my brief response as an answer he continued his odd line of questions. "Is he a gentleman of some distinction?", not really paying attention to him the clergyman continued, "is he always smartly dressed and has been known to wear a top hat?" Seeing that I wasn't really responding to his inquiries his questions changed tracks "have you known him for some time and is he a close friend?"

It was at that moment I changed my gaze from watching people enter to the person standing in front of me. Knowing he had caught my attention his face started to light up, I had only seen that particular smile a few times but I knew right away who it belonged to. "Sherlock…how good it is to see you again"…I was going to add "and what an unusual entrance" but flashing back three years and seeing him invent a Dutch bricklayers disguise this present one should have been no surprise to me.

As he sat down, Sherlock removed the elements of his facial disguise and the starched white collar that had made him appear as a man of the cloth. Then there was a type of comfortable silence between us that only close friends can share when many thoughts and feelings are expressed and exchanged when words are not necessary to convey either.

Looking at Sherlock's face I could see him deeply apologizing for his absence at John's funeral and for his choice of the solitary life he had been leading up until this moment. I tried to convey non verbally that I understood and that what had happened in the past in no way affected the friendship that had grown since our first formal introduction so many Christmas's ago.

The special moment of silent two way communication was broken when Madam Liliya Cosmina Jarkovácz, the owner, local tarot card and tea leaf reader came to our table and asked if we would be expecting anyone else to be joining us.

At that moment the name "Winfred" popped into my mind, but to madam I replied that our other guest would be joining us shortly and we would all order when she arrived. Not realizing how much time had passed since Sherlock had joined me and how little of it I had left until Winifred's arrival I tried to compress an introduction and all the events that had taken place since I had received her first distressed letter into the time available.

I started to speak when Sherlock gave me a sign to lower my voice. His cautious explanation being that "there are probably persons in this tea room that might find what you are about to share with me might be most valuable." Using a lower tone of voice that I knew would not carry much beyond the two of us I began to share what I understood and what I thought of the events that had brought him here.

During my narration Sherlock only stopped me once to ask where the Survivors list was presently located and in whose care it was. While I spoke, I watched Sherlock's interest steadily grow as I related to him the facts that I had accumulated. I was sure that what I was telling him was being combined with the information he had previously learned from his hospital visit with his brother.

I was at the point in my narrative where Winifred and I were returning from Munns which I told Sherlock is the local stationer and office supply shop and as we were both passing the dock area had witnessed a large crowd of people milling around one of the canal barges docked there. The shocking discovery we both made when I heard Winifred's voice above the general conversation in the tea room call "Mary" and saw she was looking around trying to locate the table where we were seated.

I raised my right hand enough so that it would be a beacon to guide her to the right table. As she reached her destination, removed her coat and seated herself she smiled at me.

Then seeing what for the most part appeared to be a threadbare attired gentleman seated next to her she looked at him not quite sure what to make of what she saw and quizzically asked "Mr. Holmes?"

Trusting that I had relayed enough information so that Sherlock would undertake helping me with this mystery I began formal introductions. "Winifred…this is my friend of many years Mr. Sherlock Holmes." I watched as they reached out to exchange a polite handshake and I looked into both faces trying in that short span of time to see how each might take to the other.

I could tell immediately that Winifred was in awe of Sherlock. She knew a great deal about his reputation both from what she had heard as a child and later read about as an adult in the Strand. I also had to remember it had a lot to do with what I had shared with her of the long term friendship John and I had with him before I met her. Winfred beamed and looked considerably relieved as she replied "Mr. Holmes what a pleasure to meet you."

I carried on with introductions "Sherlock, this is my good friend I met during the war, Miss Winifred Jeffery." Sherlock flashed the briefest of smiles then said "A pleasure to meet you too Miss Jeffery, although I have not read any of your mystery novels I have heard that they are well written and that you have a wide circle of devoted readers." I took this opportunity to consult the menu and my lunch companions did the same.

Witnessing the colourfully dressed owner of the Oradea tea room pass our table I caught her attention in an attempt to cover any awkward silence after the initial introductions were completed. I informed Madam Jarkovácz that the three of us were ready to order.

While we enjoyed what turned into a rather late luncheon the conversation turned to mundane matters and we steered clear of our "mystery" for some time. Inevitably the conversation eventually came around to the subject of the Survivors list. Sherlock cautiously put up his right hand and said to both of us "I think that matters concerning this particular subject are better left to a discussion in a more private setting perhaps at Miss Jeffery's home, tomorrow afternoon?

Chapter 20

At the same time Sherlock, Winifred and I were meeting at Winfred's home in regards to the Survivors list and event details there was also another meeting regarding the Survivors list taking place. That particular meeting was taking place behind closed doors at an undisclosed private gentleman's club in London. (Before I go further, it must be revealed that the information I am about to relate came to me via Mycroft Holmes.)

In a dark oak panelled room there were about twenty four men in attendance seated around a large oblong mahogany table each representing the major post war political powers. In addition there were industrialists and financiers in attendance. The following dialog I am paraphrasing came from the actual recorded minutes of this meeting. Each party in the document was referred to only as speaker 1 or speaker 2 etc. for the sake of anonymity and secrecy.

Speaker 1: "I would like to thank you gentlemen for taking the time to attend this important and somewhat urgent meeting. I would also like to extend a warm welcome to those who have made the journey from the United States of America. I trust your crossing on the Lancastria was both safe and pleasant." *As a note the RMS Lancastria is a British Cunard liner.*

"If we could all be seated we can begin. I believe that all in attendance are aware of or have some knowledge of the Survivors list, why it was created and its ultimate purpose. The list up until this point, due to its nature and content has remained a closely guarded secret known to only a select few. Due to an oversight or gross negligence if you will the list is now in the hands of a woman mystery writer who resides in Gravesend."

"The ladies name is Winfred Jeffery and if it wasn't for her damn writer's curiosity it would have been a fairly easy task to have retrieved the list when an opportunity eventually presented itself. But apparently there was a name on the list (I believe it was Mycroft Holmes) that caught her attention and because of this Miss Jeffery contacted her friend Mary Watson. Mrs. Watson resides in London and it would only be natural to contact her to see if the Holmes listed was in fact related to a more famous Holmes. Sherlock Holmes in articular who I understand has taken up bee keeping and lives in Doncaster."

Speaker 2: "Are we to assume then that this Mrs. Watson is married to a Dr. John Watson, who collaborated with the former detective on a number of cases? In other words, whether there was a connection to Sherlock Holmes or not he would probably have an interest in leaning more. His sleuthing curiosity would make him look further into something that should never have seen the light of day?"

Speaker 1: "We are aware at this point in time that Mr. Holmes is making his way to Gravesend, may in fact already have arrived to meet with both Mrs. Watson and Miss Jeffery. It appears the three have gone to great lengths to have everyone believe that this is only some sort of reunion. However, as the list has not actually been seen at this point we have have very little information to work with?"

Speaker 2: "There is another matter that should be brought up that would be the four unsuccessful attempts to retrieve the Survivors list which have resulted in a failed theft, an unsuccessful assassination and two murders. I am beginning to question if the people picked to carry out the retrieval a Mr. Thomas Malone Prescott, Mr. Andrew Foster Perry and a Miss Ashley Laurinda Taggart were as qualified as they made themselves out to be and if the fees paid for their services have been a wise investment?.

"Of the three Mr. Prescott presents the most trouble to us, in his career as a bare knuckle boxer he has gained something of a reputation for killing at least one or maybe two opponents in a match. His form of boxing which has been crudely been referred to as a no holds barred fight has resulted in the body of the loser being quickly and quietly taken care of after each fight.

"From his actions it appears that Mr. Prescott lacks both the proper finesse and skill needed to extract valuable information. In other words to kill only when absolutely necessary and if there is to be a murder to efficiently and properly dispose of the body and any evidence thereafter. A

s a result of two fruitless and bungled efforts with a (the speaker paused to look sheet of paper) Charles Slade and a Stan Mayes our Mr. Prescott has inadvertently left a visible trail of tantalizing evidence. That if I can only assume Mr. Sherlock Holmes gets sight of and decides to follow up it would eventually lead him back to the people in this very room and to the events of 1918."

Chapter 21

The next afternoon I arrived at Winfred's just a little ahead of Sherlock to retrieve the Survivors list from its hiding place and to prepare afternoon tea for the three of us. When Sherlock arrived, he removed his top hat and coat hung them up then sat down and asked to see the list.

While Winifred sat close to him watching for any sign or reaction I brought the tea to a low table beside her and started pouring. Sherlock silently scanned the list then commented "A most interesting document that has no doubt brought about some great mischief and may yet prove to be more harmful if it were allowed back into the hands of whoever created it in the first place. With what I have read and deciphered this would be a matter better suited to people who are more able to deal with these sorts of affairs."

Sherlock placed the list on his lap, turned and looked at Winfred then asked "In light of this development it should be asked if another party may be better suited to take up your case Miss Jeffery." Sherlock stated this with the finality of a man who had left his sleuthing days behind him. Holmes continued, "I believe survivors in this particular case does not refer to the remaining passengers who have found themselves involved in some maritime catastrophe but rather survivors refers to those on the list who have not yet had their name struck through with red ink and can still be counted for the moment,, as being among the living."

"Mr. Holmes you need me as much as I need you." Winifred countered. "How do you see that?" Holmes asked. "I have a problem that you now have some knowledge of. I also admit that this matter can not be solved by a literary detective. My knowledge of crime and of criminals is based solely on drawing from my life experience and whatever mystery novels may have passed before my eyes since I learned to read."

Winfred sensing she could win Sherlock with flattery continued "Mr. Holmes, we need to draw on your extensive experience of crime and criminals. Mary has shared many of your brilliant sleuthing skills during the time you worked with John." "While I am flattered with your offer Miss Jeffery, I think you would find the process easier and far less challenging if you were to consult with my brother, or perhaps you can glean some information from Watson's chronicles either through back issues of the Strand or through his printed and bound anthology."

Since the atmosphere between Sherlock and Winifred had appeared quite civil yesterday I was somewhat taken aback by his cold and almost thoughtless answer to Winfred's plea. I realized the effects the two murders were having on Winfred and decided to evoke some old memories of his time with John to see if I could convince Sherlock to change his mind and help us.

Acting as I did on the barge with Dr. Briggs I took matters into my own hands. I stood up motioned Sherlock to do the same and told Winfred that we would be back to join her shortly. Once outside her front door I looked at him as if he had lapsed back to the introverted bee keeper living in Doncaster and not the great consulting detective I had hoped was returning.

"Sherlock" I started while trying to contain my emotions and the edge creeping in my voice "didn't you once say to John, give me problems, give me work, give me the most abstruse cryptogram or the most intricate analysis and I am in my own proper atmosphere. I can dispense then with artificial stimulants.

But I abhor the dull routine of existence. I crave for mental exaltation. That is why I have chosen my own particular profession, or rather created it, for I am the only one in the world. You fully know and understand Watson that I cannot live without brain-work. What else is there to live for?"

"Your home and bees are safe and in good hands and will be there when you return to Doncaster but Winfred and I need your help very much right now." I watched the familiar face I had known for many years to see if I had reached him and had not hurt him in any way. It was as if he was lost in great thought for a moment or two when suddenly he flashed one of his famous smiles, brought his hands together and announced "Mary we must pay a visit to the local mortician tomorrow and find out in detail how two local men met their unfortunate end."

When we returned to Winifred I started to speak but Sherlock indicated he wished to go first. "Miss Jeffery I must first start by apologizing for my hasty and not too well thought out answer. Mary has pointed out that my mental skills are better suited to solving your present situation than identifying a second queen in a bee colony in order to start another hive."

"For the moment there are only two requests I will make of you." "Yes Mr. Holmes" Winifred answered greatly relieved. "First, that you place the Survivors list in my care which should deflect any further interest from you to me. Second, that you tell me all you know about this document. Every detail of where you found it and any events that have taken place since your ownership of it."

Chapter 22

In a dark oak panelled room after the debate had died down (again the following dialogue I am paraphrasing came from the actual recorded minutes of this meeting)

Speaker 3: "With our present retrieval methods bearing no fruit perhaps its time we should adopt a more basic way of dealing with this matter?"

Speaker 1: "What are you suggesting?"

Speaker 3: "Of the three, Mr. Andrew Foster Perry has proven to be the least disappointing; perhaps it is time to see if he has some skills in burglary." "We must find a way to draw all three from Miss Jeffery's residence long enough for Mr. Perry to enter the residence and hopefully retrieve the list."

A possible opportunity for this action did indeed present itself. With Sherlock and I having already made an appointment to go to Joseph Hay & Son the local mortuary to gather more facts concerning the two local deaths. As we were getting ready to leave Sherlock stated to Winifred "Miss Jeffery I certainly understand your feelings as to what you witnessed at the dock a short time ago but I believe your presence will be required. Since you are a resident of Gravesend and in some capacity knew these men you may be required to positively identify both bodies."

Watching Winifred's reaction to this grim request I placed an assuring hand on her shoulder and told her that she would only have to remain long enough to positively identify the builder and the inn keeper then she could leave the funeral home if she chose to.

The three of us were met in the appropriately lit and sombre atmosphere reception area of the funeral home. We were greeted by a tall and formally dressed young who introduced himself as Alistair Hay (who we took to be the junior Mr. Hay) "My father has already prepared the two bodies for identification and for further forensic examination as you had requested Mr. Holmes. Dr. Briggs as per your instructions is already waiting for you in the preparation room."

Lead quietly and respectably by the young funeral director we made our way past two fairly large visitation rooms that had both been set up in anticipation of receiving mourners of the deceased who would come to pay their respects. Alistair stopped in front of a door that was clearly identified with a small engraved brass plaque that stated "authorized personal only".

The young funeral director reached out and turned the door knob opening the door and stated to us "this is our preparation room, please step this way." From the low lit and warm and carpeted rooms we had been walking through previously the room we now entered was a porcelain white tiled floor and walled room. We could detect an odour of embalming chemicals in the room that was illuminated by a combination of both overhead electric light and sunlight streaming through skylights placed in the ceiling.

The three of us took in the surroundings. Clearly this was an area not seen by the public. I noticed that there were stainless steel metal shelves attached to the white tiled walls. On the shelves were tools, instruments of the trade carefully stored in their respective resting places? These items, along with chemicals were used to make the deceased presentable to the ones who had come to pay their final respects.

While all of this could be taken in and acknowledged the two white shrouded covered gurneys in the middle of the room caught and held our respective attention. All three of us being momentarily transfixed, Dr. Briggs presence did not immediately register until I heard his familiar voice with a slight echo resulting from the tile. "Mrs. Watson it is good to see you again, even if it is in such an unfortunate circumstance." Not waiting for me to make formal introductions he extended his right hand in greeting and said to Sherlock "Mr. Holmes, what a pleasure and honour to meet you in person sir.

I am Dr. Briggs and conducted the preliminary examination on both bodies" After he had heartily shaken Sherlock's hand he turned to Winifred and inquired "Miss Jeffery?' When Winfred nodded yes, the doctor gently took her hand lightly shook it twice and complimented her "It is also a pleasure to meet you in person I thoroughly enjoyed your last book The Pathway of Lost Souls."

"Before we begin can it be assumed that you all have interest in some form or another with the deceased?' Alistair Hay inquired then he continued the line of questioning "it is Miss Jeffery's interest that I am unclear with?" "Miss Jeffery's interest is the most important" stated Sherlock with some assurance "because before any type of investigation is to begin we must be assured that we have the right bodies to fit the crimes that have obviously been committed"

"Mr. Hay, if you will so kind as to pull back the shrouds so that a positive identification can be made." Sherlock instructed the young funeral director. Watching Winifred start to retreat to the door as the sheets were being pulled back, I took her hand and reassured her "Winfred all you have to do is quickly look at them to make sure it is Charles and Stan then this ordeal will be over for you.

Sherlock taking up the position at the head of each gurney looked from the uncovered faces to Winfred "Miss Jeffery if you would please" and then directed her attention to the now uncovered faces. Winfred haltingly took the few steps from the end of the gurney to the front. Still not able to face the task Sherlock took matters into his hands. He directed Winfred's attention to her left and calmly asked "The man on the left is?" Winfred looked down at the cold, colourless face that she had remembered from the examination of the devastation of St. Peter and St. Paul church and softly replied "that is Charles Slade."

Not wanting to lose momentum, Sherlock continued "The man on the right is?" Winifred feeling that her resolve was starting to fade towards the task forced herself to look at another lifeless face. Hearing his voice again caution her "Don't take too long miss; I have a feeling that some more of the roof may yet give way" as his voice faded away she softly responded that this was indeed Stan Mayes."

Out of respect for the visible signs Winfred was starting to exhibit Sherlock indicated that the two lifeless and colourless faces should be covered again. "Thank you Miss Jeffery." Sherlock looked to me to help in some way for Winfred to gather her composure "Mary, perhaps its best if you take Miss Jeffery out to the reception area until she is feeling better. Dr. Briggs, Mr. Hays and I are going to see what each body can tell us about the killer and the type of weapon that was used to carry out this gruesome task. I will share what I have learned later."

When both Winfred and I had left the bodies were fully uncovered then turned on their stomachs so that the fatal wound at the base of each neck could be examined. Even though both bodies had been in a type of cold storage to prevent decay and that most of the natural colour had now drained away from the skin, the fatal wounds still looked and presented themselves as if they had been recently inflicted.

After a moment of silence Sherlock asked "Dr. Briggs, from what you are observing could you determine the type of weapon that may have been employed?" "I would say from the dimensions and depth of the wound inflicted it was some type of cudgel Mr. Holmes. As you no doubt understand it is among the simplest of all one handed weapons.

Essentially a short staff, or stick, usually made of wood and the wounds inflicted are generally known as *bludgeoning* or blunt-force trauma injuries…in other words, fatal. As a note Mr. Holmes, when I was examining the first body on the deck of the barge I informed Mrs. Watson…*that he may have been killed before being disposed of. I surmised this while he was face down on the deck because I noticed a large contusion at the base of the skull breaking his neck. In my opinion no matter what was used to strike the killing blow the person doing it had considerable strength.*"

The last part of the doctor's statement lodged in Sherlock's mind triggering a connection which caused him to ask "Dr. Briggs what is another name for a cudgel?" Well Mr. Holmes in Ireland it is known as a shillelagh." Beginning to fit the pieces together Sherlock continued "and would you conjecture that a man who makes a living as a bare knuckle boxing might possess the required strength to deal such a fatal blow?'

Dr. Briggs not too sure where the questioning was heading answered "If he had what is a referred to as a mean right cross in boxing circles and was firmly holding a cudgel or shillelagh it is possible he could with one clean blow to the back of the neck deliver a fatal blow." "Thank you Dr. Briggs, I believe with some certainty I can identify the killer of these two men as a Thomas Malone Prescott."

Later, when we returned to Winfred's home and she was taking a much needed respite from what had been a trying experience, Sherlock shared what he had learned about the two deceased men. He related what the doctor had conjectured then started to summarize ..."All the facts I have gathered so far now seem to fit." Sherlock stood up at this point and started to pace the room. "However what we have not yet discovered is the motive for the murders.

The only connection I can see is that they had some general association with Miss Jeffery which is hardly motivation for what has occurred. Even more puzzling, is that the killer made little or no attempt to conceal his crime? This leads me to the conclusion, that Mr. Prescott has no real talent for killing outside of his chosen sport and he is under some pressure to carry out these killings as expediently as possible."

It was about 6 p.m. when Winfred, looking somewhat refreshed from her rest joined Sherlock and me to tell us that she was now feeling better and then commented that she would start to prepare the evening meal. I pointed to the range and pots seated on top already heating indicating that this task was well under way and that we would be eating shortly.

During the meal, little was discussed about the events that had unfolded other than Sherlock saying to both of us as I was removing the finished dinner plates and cutlery from the table that he was gong to take a day trip to London tomorrow to inform Mycroft of the two murders and that he fairly certain of the killers identity.

After an hour or so of light conversation Sherlock rose to leave. "I will take my leave of you both to return to my hotel to prepare for tomorrow. When I return tomorrow night I will share any new information I may have acquired." Donning his outer coat and top hat he reached into an inside pocket to assure himself that the Survivors list was still safely located there.

Confirming that it was, he flashed a brief smile in Winfred's direction 'You may rest some what assured Miss Jeffery that this matter will soon be at an end. We know of at least one suspect in this affair and with my brother's extensive knowledge we yet might find out who else is involved."

Chapter 23

The next morning three distinct events took place.

The first: Sherlock making his way from his hotel to his brother's government office in London. Winifred and I were on a less than official journey to Culverstones the local green grocer to replenish her larder.

As we entered the shop Winfred stopped for a moment and looked around as if she was still seeing of all the damage and devastation that had been repaired since her last visit. At the same time a shadowy figure that was charged with an important undertaking had remained hidden until after our departure and managed to force open a bedroom window to gain illegal entrance to Winifred's home.

"Good morning ladies and how can I help you today?" the shop keeper behind the counter cheerily greeted us as he tipped his cap in our direction. This brought Winfred back to the present and she took her shopping list from her hand bag and began the process of transferring food items from the list to the basket the shop owner had provided for his customers.

While Winfred was picking up and examining the goods the store had to offer, putting some in the basket and others back the uninvited guest was involved in a similar task. Only his actions consisted of opening and emptying drawers and cupboards taking down books from their shelves ransacking each in a desperate search for what he had instructed to find.

When we had finished shopping I suggested to Winfred that we take a walk along the high street hoping that the sights and sounds of people and commerce in Gravesend would brighten her mood. When we had walked both sides of the street and had stopped in a couple of shops that caught our interest she decided it was time to return home and prepare a late supper in anticipation of Sherlock's return from London.

When Winfred put the key in the lock and opened the front door the sight that presented its self to both of us was almost indescribable.

It was as if a violent windstorm had become trapped within the walls of her house and all the contents of drawers, cupboards and shelves had been swept up then deposited haphazardly on the floor of each room. As she entered very uncertain as to what to make of the scene I heard myself caution her "Winfred stop…don't disturb anything until Sherlock returns."

Chapter 24

"Ah Sherlock" his older brother stated while rising from his large oak desk "you have come to tell me about the two murders that have taken place in Gravesend." Sherlock briefly smiled then offhandedly said "I see you have recovered from your wound."

Mycroft moved the healed arm in acknowledgement. As both sat down Sherlock continued while putting his hat and cane beside him "Good news as well as bad reaches you fairly quickly. Yes, there were two murders committed within a few days by a Thomas Malone Prescott. I am starting to suspect that the murders, a Miss Winfred Jeffery and the Survivors list are very much linked together."

"I should ask Sherlock if this Miss Jeffery is in any danger." "No because she is in the care of Mary Watson, who is proving herself very capable in helping to seek and sort out important facts in this case." "What do know of this Thomas Prescott?" Mycroft inquired "Only for the most part what has been reported in the police gazette. Personally he proved to be something of a shadowy figure the few times in the past when Watson's, mine and Prescott's paths have crossed. The few certain facts I have about him are that he was born February 6, 1887.

Prescott's parents are from Dramorra, Ireland although he was raised in England he had a traditional Irish upbringing. He is well known throughout the borough where he resides and to the police by reputation as the "badger." A skilled expert in weapons and use of explosives I would describe him as tall and lean. His slight stature and build belay his physical strength but these features are well suited for his chosen profession as a bare knuckle prize fighter.

At that moment the same sets of thoughts ran through both brothers' minds that the man who had committed the two savage killings was also the man who had tried to assassinate Mycroft and could be responsible for the near destruction of a church.

Sherlock continued "It was said that anyone who fought the badger and lived they should consider themselves most fortunate for some of his less fortunate competitors never experienced that good providence. With the exception of you" Sherlock gestured to his brothers healed arm "in Gravesend there are two such men."

"Do you have a plan for dealing with this man, should you, Mrs. Watson or Miss Jeffery encounter him?" Mycroft asked in concern while rising from his desk indicating that the meeting was coming to an end. "Assuming he has come to reclaim this" at which time Sherlock also rose, collecting his hat and cane then momentarily producing the Survivors list "hopefully he will now assume that I am in possession of it. I will deal appropriately with Mr. Prescott as the situation presents itself."

Chapter 25

By early evening Winifred and I had been standing and waiting together on the railway station passenger platform for some time watching for the London to Gravesend trains arrival. Each of us hoping that among the passengers there would be a consulting detective who could sort out the chaos that had presented itself when Winifred had opened the door to her home earlier.

We both witnessed and heard the large and powerful steam engine like some great fire breathing Chinese dragon pass slowly by us with the line of passenger carriages it was pulling start to slow down. With the clank of buffers on buffers the train came to a stop. Almost in sequence the conductors descended from their individual carriages and started to assist passengers in moving safely from the bottom carriage step onto the station platform.

A growing and bustling impromptu ballet of passengers and luggage proceeded in front of us for a couple of minutes until we both spotted the familiar form of Sherlock starting to make his way purposefully down the passenger platform towards the station. Walking towards him Sherlock looked momentarily surprised at seeing the unexpected and welcoming committee moving towards him.

The three of us met next to a large wooden roof support post then Sherlock commented about our encounter. First he said "Mary" then "Miss Jeffery considering that the itinerary for my return journey to Gravesend it was originally planned that I was to join you both at Miss Jeffery's home I can only deduce that there has been a major development sometime during my brief visit to London." I looked to Winfred and let her share first hand what she had witnessed when she had put the key in the lock earlier then opened her front door.

As we entered Winfred's darkened home all three of us could only partially appreciate the devastation that was waiting to be fully illuminated. "I should turn on some light" Winfred stated as she stepped into the room carefully and cautiously picking her way among the strewn papers and scattered contents. Winfred turned on a couple easily reached table lamps then stood looking lost. Asking like any character from one of her mystery novels 'How are you ever going to know who did this Mr. Holmes and why?"

Sherlock already surveying the damage for possible clues smiled in Winfred's direction and assuredly stated "The why Miss Jeffery we already know, an individual or a group of individuals wishes the return of the Survivors list. I believe this needless destructive action on the part of the person who has broken into your home is proof of its importance to them. The who, will prove to be as easy. It is my experience with almost any type of crime that the one committing it takes something from the crime scene and always leaves something behind."

Sherlock made a couple of circuits of the clutter, occasionally bending down to turn over a pile of paper or rearrange another. Saying as much to himself as to us "this will take too long to look for something that may have been misplaced. What I need, is for somebody to locate an article that is out of place, something that does not belong here."

"Miss Jeffery" Sherlock said as he straightened himself "you have resided been in this house for some time to be generally familiar with most of its contents and thus should be able to spot something that might not belong."

Feeling as if she was being drawn into one of her mysteries Winfred, a little more than interested asked "Such as Mr. Holmes?" "Say a small article of clothing, some personal papers, jewellery perhaps, or in the off chance that our burglar was perhaps an intelligent educated avid reader a small easily carried book."

Winfred not believing what was happening next heard herself state "Perhaps like the one next to you on your right hand side Mr. Holmes?" Sherlock looked to his right and saw a small nondescript dark green book lying on the table as if it had placed there by its owner only momentarily to be retrieved later. The cover and the spine in faded gold letters read Foundations of Mathematics by Hilbert and Bernays.

Trembling slightly he picked up the prize and opening it scanned the inside for clues of its reader then spied an inscription on the jacket leaf and let out a great laugh of success. Both Winfred and I looked surprised at the reaction he was having.

Not keeping us in further suspense Sherlock read to us what was autographed in pencil. "To Andrew Foster Perry on his 16th birthday March 23, 1904." Putting the book down he smiled like a cat that had finally caught two troublesome mice and pointed in the general direction to the chaos on the floor and stated to both of us "now we have two."

Chapter 26

Andrew Foster Perry returned empty handed to London and to number 15 Exton Street with only a small suitcase containing a few personal items and a change of clothes. Other than not being able to locate the list he had been instructed to locate in the mystery writers home his only other worry was where he had misplaced his copy of Foundations of Mathematics.

Until he was contacted by the anonymous people who gave instruction for any further assignments for him or for himself or Ashley, Andrew decided it was probably wiser to restrict his travels between the Brixton Market and his favourite pub The Prince Albert, both being within a close proximity to his home.

For those who have not been to this part of the city Brixton Market comprises a street market in the center of Brixton, south London, England, and the adjacent covered market areas in nearby arcades Reliance Arcade, Market Row and Granville Arcade.

The Market began on Atlantic Road in the 1870s and subsequently spread to Brixton Road which had a very wide footway. Brixton then was a rapidly expanding London railway suburb with newly opening shops, including the first branch of David Greig at 54-58 Atlantic Road in 1870, and England's first purpose-built department store, Bon Marché, on Brixton Road in 1877. The market is a popular attraction, with lower class shoppers being entertained by street musicians.

If you prefer genteel shopping then Brixton Market is not the place for you. With the many sights and smells of large hanging meat carcasses jostling against stalls full of ten penny shoes, tin pots and pans, local cheese, baked goods of all types, large propped up open rough hewn wooden boxes over flowing with local vegetables and fruit and chicken wire crates full of a variety of objecting poultry and fowl the loud, pushy vendors yelling their wares in a collection South London, Cockney, German, Polish, Italian accents trying to entice the large throngs of curious buyers browsing the abundant stands to buy their goods.

The Prince Albert pub, located on the corner of Coldharbour Lane and the High street was an established medium sized local and well known institution frequented by a mix of working class men, residents living within the vicinity and petty criminals. Andrew knew he could go there for a peaceful pint of beer and a meal of fish and chips and not feel as if he had to quickly wolf down both while looking over his shoulder to see if he was being pursued by an angry creditor or by a constable on the beat.

Besides being a place for drink and food the Prince Albert also acted as an unofficial post office where Andrew could retrieve unmarked anonymous envelopes from the inn keeper containing assignments. The enclosed instructions told him where to go and what clandestine task needed to be carried out.

After a particular trying argument during a meagre supper with his parents about money owed to help pay the rent Andrew decided to go out into evening to drown his sorrows at the Prince Albert pub.

As he passed the large Brixton Market most of the overhead electric lighting had been turned off. Shoppers with their purchases had long since left the area leaving only the vendors their final task of closing up and securing darkened stalls to prepare for the next day.

Andrew angry at himself for forgetting his favourite book and infuriated about his parents hounding him for money stayed at the Prince Albert drinking his problems away all the while hoping that the inn keeper wasn't keeping too close an eye on a growing unpaid pub tab. When he heard the call "last round" Andrew hoped what he had consumed during the evening in the pub would at least keep all his troubles at bay until tomorrow.

Whether he had left the Prince Albert to return home after an evening of drinking or had taken a late solitary night walk through Brixton all of the failed thief's troubles ended before he ever reached 15 Exton Street. With a decisive and killing blow to the back of his head delivered by an unseen assailant employing an Irish instrument of death. The killer on instructions had been waiting some time hidden in the dark shadows of a shuttered market stand waiting for his victim to pass by.

Andrew groaned only slightly in response to the precise strike then with the sound of a skull being separated from its spine his crumpled dead body fell to the ground in the same manner as two others from Gravesend had when they had been dispassionately put to death.

Chapter 27

In a dark oak paneled room this time with fewer in attendance (as before, the following dialogue I am paraphrasing came from the actual recorded minutes of the meeting.)

Speaker 3: "Gentlemen, I'm afraid I bring bad news from Gravesend." "What bad news" asked the others?

Speaker 3: "Our Mr. Perry has failed us on two points. First, he was unable to locate the Survivors list in the mystery writer's home and at the same time he inadvertently left behind a calling card in the form of a favourite book. Knowing of Mr. Holmes legendary deduction skills upon finding the aforementioned article it would only be a matter of time until he tracks Mr. Perry down."

Speaker 4: "Can all present in this room hopefully assume then that this matter has been taken care of?"

Speaker 3: "Concerning Mr. Perry yes, the person who dealt with the first two in Gravesend has also dealt with him in Brixton but as to locating the book no. If by some chance Mr. Holmes draws enough clues from it that brings him to the centre of this he will be dealt with by this person too."

Speaker 4: sounding somewhat frustrated "None of these endeavours have brought us any closer to our objective of retrieving the list, we are fortunate that the President of the United States and our Prime minister are at this time unaware that we have lost the list but it will only be a matter of time until they find out.

Considering that the dust of 1918 has finally started to settle I think that none of us present want to open up old wounds and return to hostilities by the list somehow being made public."

Speaker 2: "Then I can see gentlemen we have one last course of action to take, it will be somewhat drastic and may involve some risk but we are going to have to take steps to bring Miss Jeffery to London to persuade her in person hopefully with reasonable methods to turn over the list to us.

Speaker 1: "Are you suggesting we kid nap the woman against her will? That would have Mr. Holmes on our trail like the hounds that have caught scent of the fox."

Speaker 2: "No nothing that drastic, I believe that she is a reasonable woman and with Mr. Prescott's and Miss Taggart's help she may be persuaded to make the journey. As it turned out before this plan could be implemented some legal intervention was required.

Chapter 28

Magistrates' court or court of petty session is the lowest level of court in England and Wales. A magistrates' court is presided over by a tribunal consisting of three justices of the peace (also known as magistrates) or by a district judge, and dispenses summary justice, under powers usually defined by statute. The tribunal presiding over the Court is commonly referred to simply as the Bench.

When a defendant first appears before a magistrates' court, they will do so in one of three circumstances. They will either appear on bail having been charged with an offence and compelled to attend court under penalty; in response to a summons, which requires attendance but does not, in the first instance, carry any penalty for non-attendance; or in custody, having been refused bail by the police. If the defendant is on bail, she/he must first surrender to the custody of the court.

Whichever the circumstance, the first requirement is to identify him/herself to the Court. Once the Court is satisfied as to the identity of the defendant, it must consider the charges. If the charge(s) is a summary offence, the Court will generally expect a plea to be taken. If the plea is one of "not guilty", the Court will fix a date for trial, taking into account the number and availability of the witnesses.

In the City of London Magistrates' Court located 1 Queen Victoria Street London a lanky lone male defendant stood sullenly before the three magistrates. The most senior magistrate looked first at the defendant then to the documents in front of him. He cleared his throat and in a judicial sounding voice said "For the record state your name and present address." "Thomas Malone Prescott, number 22 Margate Road, Brixton." Looking again at the defendant then to the relevant records the magistrate continued. "Thomas Malone Prescott you are charged with the offence of personal assault causing bodily harm and with the offence and of wilful destruction private property, how do you plead?"

In Highbury Corner Magistrates' Court located at 51 Holloway Road much the same scene was being played out only the defendant was a fatally attractive and defiant female. "For the record miss state your name and present address." "Ashley Laurinda Taggart…51 Welbury Street, Hackney." Before continuing the magistrate looked surprised to see someone like Ashley in court, not sure why such an innocent should be here. He resumed, "Ashley Laurinda Taggart you are charged with the offence of theft with burglary on the basis of trespass and with the offence of carrying a concealed weapon with intent to cause harm, how do you plead?"

In the event of a plea of guilty, the Court will then consider sentence. For the most minor offences (or with what are treated as minor offences) where the appropriate sentence is one of a fine or discharge, this will usually follow immediately after the plea of guilty. However, where the offence is more serious and may justify a curfew, or imprisonment. Magistrates have the power to impose sentences of up to six months imprisonment for one either-way offence, and to impose consecutive sentences for multiple either-way offences up to a maximum of twelve months.

On previous instructions from powerful individuals the magistrates would never know the existence of both defendants' appointed barristers rose while indicating for their client to remain silent and seated addressed each charge then summed up with "Your worships this is my clients first offence (which in fact it wasn't) and pleads guilty to all charges. Further he/she regrets his /her actions and wishes to make full restitution for all personal and property damage they may have incurred in consideration of a fine and possible suspended sentence. In Highbury Corner Magistrates Court one of the magistrates asked "As to Miss Taggart's concealed weapon?" The answer was "It was surrendered upon her arrest your worship."

The magistrates in both courts having also being previously instructed without the knowledge of the barristers about both Thomas and Ashley in an act of believing the sincerity of the directed barristers and the silent innocence of the defendants as final judgement imposed a curfew on Thomas and Ashley that neither had any intention of ever obeying, a modest fine that they would never pay and that each compensate all the injured and wronged parties which they would never do.

The final barrister client transaction to take place that day as all were leaving their respective courts was for Thomas and Ashley each to be handed a letter sized blank white sealed envelope containing instructions pertaining to Winfred that she be persuaded to come in their company to London, of her own free will or against it and that she willingly on her arrival surrender the Survivors list or that it be taken forcibly from her.

Chapter 29

While Winfred and I were engaged in restoring her thoroughly ransacked home Sherlock made his way to the local telegraph office to enquire of his older brother what he knew about the owner of the discovered book or the book itself.

Later in the day just as we were finishing getting the house back into order, collecting piles of scattered papers form the floor, placing books back on their respective shelves and making her writing desk look more like a place to compose mysteries again, Sherlock returned. He said a quick hello to Winfred then indicated that he wish to talk to me in private. After I assured Winfred that whatever information Sherlock had acquired we would share as much as he could with her I joined Sherlock near the front door.

While removing his coat and hat he began with"This is much more sinister than we can imagine." Sherlock then handed me the telegram he had received from London. It turned out that Andrew Foster Perry, 32 (the owner of the lost book) born March 23, 1888, who had resided at 15 Exton Street had been found lying dead in the street early in the morning by a Brixton market stall proprietor.

I put the telegram down for a minute looked at Sherlock and stated "Why that means." " Yes, that means that Mr. Perry's services were brutally terminated shortly after his arrival in London from Gravesend for his failure to locate this." And again Sherlock pulled the Survivors list from his pocket.

Looking at me, Sherlock indicated that there was more to be read. Picking up the telegram I continued. It turned out that Mr. Perry had been killed in the same manner (or style) as the two who had been murdered in Gravesend.

Out of genuine fear for Winifred's welfare I asked "Do you think that Winfred is facing any real danger because of what has happened?" He flashed one of his trademark brief smiles, then cautiously in a low voice said "because it turns out that there is a criminal connection between the deceased Mr Perry and Mr Prescott our killer it would be well that when Miss Jeffery steps outdoors for any reason that she be in the company of one of us at all times."

Sherlock took the telegram from me, started folding it to put back in his pocket then almost as an after thought unfolded it read it then surprisingly like a magician pulling a rabbit from a top hat he said "from my brother's telegram I have reason to believe that the young lady at the Spring fete held on Saturday, May 15 at the Gordon Gardens who attempted to rob Miss Jeffery of the contents of her hand bag could be an Ashley Laurinda Taggart. If this is the same person because she has a criminal connection to both Mr Perry and Mr Prescott it would be prudent that whoever keeps watch on Miss Jeffery also minds the people she may accidentally come in contact with.

Chapter 30

In a dark oak paneled room in early evening (as before, I am paraphrasing from the actual recorded minutes of this meeting). Speaker one "That will be all Peterson and close the doors on your way out" The older of the two lone occupants stated to their server then remained silent until the man addressed withdrew and the solid sound of heavy doors being closed indicated that the two lone occupants of the room had total privacy.

Speaker one: as he took out a cigar from a nearby humidor clipped the end then lit it asked "I trust that all went to plan this morning at the City of London Magistrates' Court and at Highbury Corner Magistrates' Court."

Speaker two: "The good news is that the barristers we engaged and instructed performed their legal duty as did the presiding magistrates and both Mr. Prescott and Miss Taggart are free of all charges and will be able to escort Miss Jeffery with the Survivors list back to London soon. There has been a set back though."

Speaker one: "Concerning?"

Speaker two: "Our Mr. Perry."

Speaker one: "I think I already know, the book Mr. Perry left at Miss Jefferies home has been discovered by the intrepid detective and through his older brother Mycroft, Mr. Holmes has no doubt linked the deceased Mr. Perry to Mr. Prescott and possibly to Miss Taggart."

Speaker one: "There are no known photographs with the exception of the police, that Mr. Holmes could have access too so he could identify either Mr. Prescott or Miss Taggart on sight should he see either one of them in Gravesend?"

Speaker two: "No, but Miss Jeffery while at the spring fete had enough time to look at Miss Taggart and might remember and recognize her."

Speaker one: "It's clear then as to how we will approach this matter. There can be no doubt what Mr Holmes and probably now Mrs Watson suspect. I believe Miss Jeffery will now be escorted at all times when outdoors by either or both of them. It will be Miss Taggart's task to remove the blind so to speak, being either in the form of Mr Holmes or Mrs Watson then Mr Prescott's task to secure the prey."

Chapter 31

Despite the three terrible murders that had taken place at the hand of one individual since Winifred had discovered the Survivors list the next part of this account would prove to be the most terrifying for her, troubling for me and the most challenging for Sherlock to unravel and solve.

Winifred unknowingly had become the determined focus of a group of powerful and influential men who because of past failed attempts would now stop at anything to retrieve the telling document. They had to assure that it would never fall into the wrong hands or see the light of day again and that the temporary owner could never speak of having it.

By now, both Sherlock and I had spent some considerable time in Gravesend since his arrival from Doncaster and mine from London. It was during supper one evening that Sherlock calmly announced that since the investigation could not proceed any further at this time he would return first to London to see how his brothers wound was healing, then home to his bees in Doncaster.

Upon hearing this news I noted that both Winifred's knife and fork drop to her dinner plate and a sudden look of panic played across her face.

It was as if a lifeline had been violently pulled from her grasp. Sherlock momentarily reacted to Winfred's response and to put her mind at ease calmly stated "Miss Jeffery, let me assure you that you have not been abandoned. I leave you for the moment with three certainties." "One" at this point he raised the index finger of his right hand "the list which has caused many problems will accompany me back to London where Mycroft may be able to find out more about it and its origins."

"Two" at which the finger beside went up "You will be in the competent care and protection of Mary who has proven herself to be more than capable and I trust will see that no harm comes to you until this matter how ever it plays out is finished" It was with this compliment I smiled and thanked Sherlock in my mind for imparting to me a responsibility he once would have given John to carry out.

"Three" and the third and final finger was raised "I will leave you both with Mycroft's private office address and his club where he can be contacted and a priority message may be delivered to him immediately should a situation arise that requires my attention here in Gravesend. "If" Winfred gasped…Sherlock continued "If I have gone on to Doncaster, my older brother although an arm chair expert in the arts and skills of detective work will immediately contact me then proceed in my place to expertly assist you until my return."

The next morning after Sherlock had checked out of the George Inn the three of us met at the train station to see him off on the outbound train. Again, to assure Winifred, Sherlock indicated that the Survivors list was on his person, he then handed both of us a folded piece of paper on which was written his brothers contact information then guaranteed that she (Winfred) was in good hands while I was with her.

As we watched Sherlock ascend into the railroad carriage that would take him to London, disembarking was a bare knuckle prize fighter and competent female pick pocket that unlike most did not have anyone waiting to warmly greet them on the platform. Instead the tow of them made their way from the train to the station with obvious purpose.

Chapter 32

Unexpectedly seeing his younger brother being escorted through the busy smoking lounge by a porter Mycroft arose from the green leather bound wing back chair that was a part of the sedate furnishings of the Diogenes club and asked. "Sherlock you are back early. Does your visit indicate that this business in Gravesend has come to an end?"

"No" Sherlock replied "but as there have been no further developments I have come to see if you can provide a link to the three deaths that have taken place in relation to this list." Both now seated Sherlock produced the troublesome document and passed it to Mycroft. Mycroft scanning the hand written list and occasionally shaking his head without looking up asked "And how is Miss Jeffery, I trust she is safe?" "I left her in the care of Mary Watson and since I am in possession of what might have been the cause for at least two of the deaths I believe she will be safe."

Mycroft rested the list on his lap then asked "How long will you be staying in London and do you have some place to stay?" Before Sherlock could answer either question Mycroft pressed on "the reason I ask is that I have recently come across some privileged and confidential information that may shed some light on this" at which time he pointed to the list.

"Can you leave the list with me and come to my office tomorrow afternoon at 2 p.m.?" Sherlock flashed one of his trademark smiles and answered if I leave the Lancaster Gate Hotel at 1:30 p.m. I will arrive at your office at 2 p.m.

The next afternoon just as the mantle clock chimed 2 p.m. there was a polite knocking on Mycroft's office door. A male voice on the other side announced "There is a Mr Holmes to see you sir." As Mycroft was getting up from behind his large office desk and proceeding to the door he answered "Show him in Arthur." The door opened fully and Sherlock accompanied by the male secretary entered the spacious room. As Sherlock made his way to the first available chair on the other side of his brothers office desk the secretary asked "Shall I serve the coffee now?"

When the coffee, biscuits and the tray they had been served on had been dispensed with Mycroft locked the door to his office then shared with Sherlock the information he had learned concerning the Survivors list.

I would share with the reader the nature, seriousness and severity of the information that Sherlock learned that afternoon within the secure confines of his brother's office. However due to its sensitive content, confidential nature and negative implications the information presented must remain with only the concerned parties. At the time I was informed as I was beginning to write this journal that THE OFFICIAL SECRETS ACT OF 1920 had been invoked and I would not be allowed to divulge any information under penalty of law.

What little I can share concerned the government of the United States, the United Kingdom. The Weimar Republic the people of all three countries who did not want to get involved in the Great War and those who did and why

When the formal conference had ended Mycroft asked "Will you be staying on in London for very much longer?" Sherlock answering as he started to rise from his chair "Only long enough to visit the better book shops to increase my bee keeping library." "And about Gravesend?" inquired Mycroft as he was also rising from his chair and making his way to the office door to unlock and open it.

"I believe that with the list in your permanent possession, Miss Jeffery can go back to writing her mystery novels and when the time is right, Mary can confidently return to London." "There is one thing." Sherlock said as they were now both making their way to the lobby in order for Mycroft to see Sherlock off. "What's that?" Mycroft returned. "Before I left Gravesend I informed both Miss Jeffery and Mary Watson that if there should be any developments in this matter and I was back in Doncaster to contact you."

Chapter 33

It was an event that happened two days after Sherlock's departure that would be the closest to fulfilling Madam Liliya Cosmina Jarkovácz's (the owner of the Oradea tea room), local tarot card and tea leaf readers warning to Winifred *"Something frightful will happen to you soon." Madam had began ominously while staring into the tea cup the fortune reader had then swirled the remaining cold tea in the cup and continued on "you will experience a bad shock but will not be seriously harmed in any way. After this event has come to pass your life will be in constant danger from sinister forces by something that will come into your possession"*…only the last part of the prediction had been wrong. Winfred and I were about to find out just how wrong.

As Winifred was finishing washing the breakfast dishes on that particular morning and while I was tidying up the last of the evidence of a recent break in, she stopped her chore turned slightly in my direction and commented "Mary, I have to go to Munn's this afternoon to purchase some type writer ribbon if I am to finish The Unicorn and the Wasp. I must get the manuscript sent on to be edited." Remembering my promise to Sherlock and also trying not to sound too over protective I replied "Then I will join you. I want to stop in at Warwick Antiques and Collectables (which wasn't too far from Winifred's stationers) to see if I can find a pale horse to match the one I already have."

Keeping my voice light I finished with "While you are purchasing something from the present I shall be purchasing something from the past."

The plan for the afternoon was a simple one. Winfred and I would walk together to Munn's where I would leave her safely in the shop for a short time and when she was finished she would join me in the antiques and collectables shop. Once we had finished our shopping and had returned to her home, Winfred would go back to her typewriter and I would start the evening meal.

At this time of day there any number of pedestrians and potential customers were making their way up and down the high street, some entering and exiting the various shops, others just stopping to peer into shop windows to see the goods and services offered. If I had known the identity of one particular "window shopper" (a petite build and short stature…full figured, long raven black hair and dark soul less eyes who was 27, born September 30, 1893) I would not have fallen into her well laid trap but instead kept walking.

Just as we were approaching Munn's the young lady appeared to "trip" then fall in front of Winfred and me in the process managed to scatter most of the contents of her hand bag at my feet. Still not knowing her true identity I asked as I lowered myself to her if she was alright.

Picking herself up she superficially examined herself for injuries that did not exist..."I am unhurt" she innocently answered "but could you please assist me in gathering the contents of my hand bag?" I noticed that I was more involved in the recovery process then she was when Winfred looked at me and asked if she could assist.

As I had not idea this "recovery" was part of some elaborate plan, I told Winfred the situation was well in hand and for her to go on to Munn's and I would see her shortly in the antiques and collectable store. The last I would see of Winfred as I momentarily looked up was as she was making her way to the stationers shop.

It was an odd thing when I think of the event later but as Winifred was leaving the progress of the recovery seems to have slowed down because as contents were being returned to the hand bag an impromptu inventory was now taking place.

Finally when the last item was returned and accounted for by their owner I rose to my feet and assisted the young lady to do the same. Quickly looking down the street I assumed that Winifred was still engaged with the shop owner of Munn's or purchasing additional stationary supplies.

As I was bidding my farewells the young lady coyly said "thank you Miss" and gave me a smile that a predator might give to its captured prey. Much as Winfred had experienced earlier at the fete in that simple act, it felt as if an icicle had been run up and down my spine too. It was as I was turning away that her stature manner and behaviour made me wonder if this was the same young lady that Winfred had encountered.

With a growing sense of ill ease I thought I would go to Munn's first before going to my shop. Should Winfred still be there I could explain my presence with a simple "are you ready to go?" I walked the short distance and entered the shop expecting to see Winfred engaged in literary conversation with the shop keeper or at the counter paying for her purchases. When I entered there was only one customer of the opposite sex who was busy looking at typewriters and only a young clerk behind the counter restocking shelves.

Taking in the scene and realizing she wasn't there I was now overwhelmed with panic and worry. Making my way to the counter and attracting the clerk's attention away from his task while trying to remain calm I enquired if a woman of Winfred description had been in the shop. The clerk thought for a moment then replied "yes Miss, you must have passed her because she and a gentleman left the shop together just a short time ago." Fearing the impossible I asked him to describe the gentleman. "He was a tall, a wiry sort of person, with red hair." A dreadful fear suddenly washed over me. Perhaps Winfred had been taken against her will and might come to some terrible harm.

Chapter 34

With a vague sense of unease but realizing the case could not be further investigated at this time Sherlock checked out of his London hotel, left the Survivors list with his brother and made his way back to the cottage locally known as the Beeches. He arrived just in time to harvest the latest yield from his social insect workers all the while unaware of what had taken place in Gravesend.

Leaving the location where I had hoped to meet Winifred I formulated the only plan I could to try and locate her. I entered every shop along both sides of the high street asking word for word the question I had asked at Munn's. With each negative response my heart sunk slightly lower.

Finally as a last resort I made my way to the train station to ask almost anyone if they had seen Winifred with her possible kidnapper.

As I entered the station I felt with the ebb and flow of constantly changing passengers and people coming and going my search among them would be fruitless. Thinking as John would in this situation I looked for and sought out the one logical person who might be of some help the station master. "Sorry miss, but with the number of people that come through this train station each day it's hard to remember one from another."

Seeing my obvious disappointment in his answer he half half-heartedly suggested I should inquire of the luggage handlers outside on the passenger platform. "They see more of the passengers getting off and on train's than I do." Thinking that this avenue of questioning might also be a dead end and that I might have lost Winfred the next man I interrupted from his work loading a baggage cart, told me to "ask Bill."

Bill a man in his late 40's of average height with the build of a person who looked like he would be able to load and unload baggage of all weight and size replied while stacking luggage on the cart next to him. "Why yes miss, I saw the lady in the company of the very man you described, she didn't seem very happy, perhaps a little distressed. Although the welfare of passengers is not my worry I felt that I wanted to ask if I could help. But the man looked like he could knock me down and I would stay down if I was to interfere. Feeling as if I had a possible lead I asked what train he had seen Winfred and her unwelcome companion board. "The out bound train to London." he replied.

Chapter 35

The Marconi Wireless Telegraph and Signal Company
Gravesend, Kent

Priority Message

To: Mycroft Holmes

I am contacting you in regards to a possible abduction of Winfred Jefferies by an unknown person who may have a connection to the Survivors list (stop) I believe she and her abductor are making their way to an undisclosed location in London (stop) I will shortly be leaving Gravesend and making my way to meet with you at the address your brother provided to seek your assistance (stop) Please contact Sherlock and advise him of the present situation (stop)

Mary Watson

London District Telegraph Company
90 Cannon Street, London

To: Mrs. M. Watson

I have received your message and at your request I have contacted my younger brother to inform him of the present situation and further have advised his immediate return to London (stop) I will schedule a meeting at my office when you both have arrived (stop) I cannot impress upon you enough the sensitive nature this matter has taken with the possible abduction of Miss Jeffery (stop) Your transportation from the train station has been arranged (stop)

M Holmes

Chapter 36

I didn't know all of the details of Winfred's abduction at the time, but that she was not in the shop when my "distraction" was taking place. I would hear about it only after the entire affair had been dealt with. As I had related earlier, our plan for the afternoon was simple. Winfred and I would walk together to Munn's where I would leave her safely in the shop for a short time and when she was finished she would join me in the antiques and collectables shop. Once we had finished our shopping and had returned home, Winfred would go back to her typewriter and I would start the evening meal.

As I bent down to assist the young lady I felt it was secure enough for Winfred to take the short journey from where we had been stopped to the stationers. Winfred reading my expression and hearing my words felt safe in doing this. But by this time the trap had been set. Winfred tells me as she entered Munn's there was only her and the clerk in the shop.

He greeted her with a friendly "good morning" and asked if she needed any assistance to which she replied courteously "not at this time thank you." Looking around and taking in all the stationary products the shop stocked she saw a display of the new Royal 10 upright typewriters and went over to look at them. She never saw or heard Thomas come up quietly behind her and his barely audible voice in her left ear saying in a sinister way "are you aware that a woman's neck breaks far easier than a mans neck and requires less force to do so."

Now that he had her terrified attention he gave her instructions that they would leave Munn's without raising any suspicion after which Winifred and her abductor after exited the shop and began to journey in the opposite direction to where I was engaged and distracted. They then proceeded to the train station.

When Winifred and Thomas (her abductor) arrived at the Gravesend train passenger platform they were met by Ashley (the one who had provided the necessary distraction). Both turning aside for a moment they exchanged a few words but kept their captive in sight. Then Thomas after consulting the platform clock indicated it was time for the three to board the train.

As they were seating themselves and the train started moving Winifred was being made to take the window seat with Thomas beside her and Ashley sitting facing her. Terrified she had a thousand questions she wanted to ask but remembering her abductors chilling voice in her ear thought better of it.

As more coal was being fed into the boiler and the train picked up speed Winfred silently looked over her left shoulder and out the carriage window to watch the passing buildings and the houses that comprised Gravesend ever quickly transition into a passing rolling country side and fields of crops that surrounded the town.

The only sounds she had for companionship were murmured incomprehensible bits of conversation from the other passengers, the reverberation of the carriage wheels travelling along on the rails disrupted by the occasional clatter as the train's wheels announced that it and the engine had passed over a set of points.

While the silent journey continued Winifred gradually got to know her possible destination because each time the conductor passed by to announce the next stop she knew she was getting closer to London. Winfred's uncertainty and anxiety were momentarily relieved when the conductor came through the carriage announcing "St. Pancreas station. Next stop St. Pancreas station all passengers for this station please collect your personal belonging before leaving the train."

The train slowed down with the sounds of the carriage wheel air brakes being applied it came to a final stop on the tracks with in the interior of the large and busy covered station concourse. Inside the carriage waiting for all the other passengers to leave first Thomas arose from his seat then silently indicated for Winifred to do so. When Ashley stood up and preceded to the exit Winfred exited and Thomas followed.

As the three made their way as inconspicuously as possible trying to blend in while going through and around the noisy multitude of passengers with their luggage and the stations employees they assumed they had gone unnoticed.

Unknown to both abductors two pairs of trained eyes among the anonymous many had noticed the unusual trio pass by and that the taller woman with them appeared to be distressed. This incident would be reported to the appropriate authority later.

Finally breaking free of the throng of passengers the three made their way to a nearby street exit once outside Thomas hailed a motor taxi. When one stopped at the curb Ashley entered first then Winfred and lastly Thomas. As Thomas solidly closed the taxi door the driver asked "Where to sir?" Thomas leaned forward and in a low voice that only the driver could hear gave him the address f an obscure nondescript building located in Stepney in the East end of London.

Stepney is a district of the London Borough of Tower Hamlets in London's East End that grew out of a medieval village around St Dunstan's church and the 15th century ribbon development of Mile End Road. The area built up rapidly in the 19th century, mainly to accommodate immigrant workers and displaced London poor, and developed a reputation for poverty, overcrowding, violence and political dissent

Chapter 37

I had been awake for about an hour enjoying the last part of a light breakfast while appreciating the early morning view out of the balcony doors of my hotel room (the Lancaster Gate Hotel) when I heard a soft knock on the door. When I went to open it there stood a smartly dressed young bell hop holding a silver tray in his right hand. "A message for you Miss" I smiled at his assumption removed the envelope and then left a gratuity in its place. Assuming that I was going to open the envelope and read the note in his presence...he inquired "Will there be an answer?"

Remembering Mycroft's cautioning in his telegram to me I politely said "no" and continued "if there is I will leave it at the front desk to be delivered."

Thanking the messenger and closing the door I carried the envelope and went back to my breakfast. While drinking the last of my morning coffee I looked at the place setting in front of me hoping to find something suitable that could be employed as a letter opener. Cleaning the butter knife with a napkin I slit open the envelope curious as to the identity of the sender. As soon as I unfolded the note inside I realized from the hand writing that the correspondent was Sherlock.

Mary:

It seems that I have had to leave my bees to their own devices yet again having received a message from Mycroft. I arrived in London from Doncaster yesterday afternoon. I contacted my brother last night and you and I have an appointment with him today at (here Sherlock gave the time). To this end I have arranged for a motor taxi, with destination instructions previously relayed to the driver, He will be waiting to take you from your hotel to the address that houses Mycroft's office where you and I shall meet.

I was shocked to learn from Mycroft that Miss Jeffery has been abducted. I fear for her safety when it is discovered that she does not have the Survivors list with her. There is however some good news in all of this. Two persons in the employ of my brother witnessed Miss Jeffery in the company of a distinctive looking man and an attractive young woman leaving the Gravesend train at the St. Pancreas station and making their way from the station concourse to a street exit.

There is a reasonable chance with the descriptions provided that Mycroft may know the identity of at least one or possibly both of the persons involved and if that is the case, this evidence should provide a suitable lead which will be pursued. Be assured that both Mycroft and I will pool all of our resources to rescue Miss Jeffery and have her safely returned unharmed to Gravesend.

Sherlock

Chapter 38

There were not any witnesses in the area when a motor taxi stopped in front of WH Matthews & Co which presented its self as a Residential Conveyancing office located at 109 Old Street, Stepney, and London. Three passengers silently left the vehicle and entered the building.

Here I would like to include Winifred's account of details of her abduction.

Although I suspected this abduction had a great deal to do with the survivors list I had no way of confirming this information much less who my abductors were. My confusion became greater as the three of us left the motor taxi which had transported us from the train station. We now entered an unlit office. Every surface in the entire area including papers, documents, chairs, desks and filing cabinets were covered in a thick layer of dust which filled me with a sense of foreboding.

Walking through the abandoned workplace felt as if we might be disturbing long departed ghosts. We then entered via a door at the rear of the office and transitioned from a room of neglect to a well lit, dark oak panelled room with a mahogany table and seating for what looked to be approximately twenty four persons.

My captors remained stationary and silent as if they had completed their task and were awaiting further instructions. About a minute later a distinguished looking man (who did not introduce himself) entered the room assessed the situation then said "Thomas and Ashley well done. You may leave now. Your payments will be deposited in the usual manner tomorrow morning."

With the dismissal of my abductors and realizing that I was alone the gentleman in front of me gave me a cold look as he said "Miss Jeffery" here he indicated a seat next to me "please be seated. It has come to our attention that you have come into possession of a document that does not belong to you and we would like to have returned" I felt as if all of the blood in me had just drained to my feet.

Chapter 39

That afternoon at the time Sherlock had appointed in his note, I left the motor taxi and met him on the front steps of the building that housed his brother's office. Sensing my urgency we dispensed with polite small talk and hastily made our way to Mycroft's chambers.

In the outer office we were met by a male secretary who introduced himself to us as "Arthur". "I will let Mr Holmes know you have arrived." Getting up from his desk he went to the door that lead to the inner office, knocked softly and announced "Sir, Mr Holmes and Mrs Watson to see you."

The sound coming from the other side of the door indicated someone rising from a chair. Sherlock heard the familiar sound of his brothers voice say "Show them in Arthur." As we were being lead into the inner office I was impressed by the scale of the room, indicating to me that the elder Holmes must be a man of great power, importance and influence.

Dismissing the secretary and taking the initiative towards formal greetings Mycroft moved in my direction extended his hand and while gentle shaking it stated "It is a pleasure to meet you Mrs Watson I do however wish it was under better circumstances." To his younger brother there were no words of greeting but only of fact. "Sherlock I believe I have been able to make a connection between Miss Jefferies abductors and the Survivors list."

"Please be seated" he indicated the two chairs in front of his desk. Before Mycroft resumed he went to the desk opened a drawer and removed a document. "This record…this Survivors list" Mycroft retrieved the document from the drawer "if it was to fall in the wrong hands could undo the relative peace the world has enjoyed since the end of the war. It could also expose why certain countries who claimed neutrality at the start and during the hostilities entered into a conflict that in no way affected them."

"It could call into question the leadership and government of certain countries and cast doubt on whose best interest they were acting." "Not to mention" Mycroft continued "the actions and motives of industries and businesses of these countries. Those who stood to benefit and make a profit from the fighting. I think with this information that you both would agree that it was important enough and sensitive enough to protect at all cost." I nodded in agreement. Sherlock showed little reaction to this revelation and it made me wonder if he had faced a situation like this before.

Sitting down at his desk Mycroft continued "We now have the what, now as to the matter of the who. During the war I placed teams of operatives in all of the major train stations to keep a watch on arriving out of town passengers to see whether their actions or interactions warranted further attention and follow up.

This how I knew of the arrival of a young patent clerk who had come to London seeking your help Sherlock during the war before Doctor and Mrs. Watson had." I momentarily flashed back to the first meeting the three of us had with Mr. Einstein and was impressed with Sherlock's brother for site and talent. Obviously the brothers had more than a last name in common and I felt he could bring about a rescue for Winifred.

Returning the Survivors list to a drawer Mycroft continued. "Despite the war being over and considering the terms of the armistice that was applied to certain countries I felt it was prudent to continue the surveillance. Why? Because I felt there would always be governments and countries that might remain hostile to the United Kingdom and might want to do some harm or redress old perceived injuries. It was this thinking that allowed me to pass along the information concerning Miss Jeffrey."

"My two operatives at St. Pancreas station had recognized Miss Jeffery from her books and took down great detail of the man and women she was seen leaving the train and station with. The man from their description is Thomas Malone Prescott, 33 years of age. Although they only had a short time to observe him they described him as tall, lean and wiry, malevolent looking man with shocking red hair and beard. From previous information gathered we know he is a skilled expert in weapons and the use of explosives."

"It has always been noted that anyone who had fought him and lived should consider them selves most fortunate, for some of his competitors never experienced that good providence. We believe because of his skills that Mr. Prescott is the prime suspect in the two murders that took place in Gravesend and the one that took place in Brixton Market here in London."

Like a hound that had just caught the possible scent of the fox Sherlock asked "where does this Mr. Prescott reside?" "Number 22, Margate Road, Brixton and he has been seen in and around the area of the East India Docks."…"and the lady?"

"Ashley Laurinda Taggart, 27 years of age, has a petite build and short stature with long raven black hair. Of the two, she is the most dangerous because she possesses a devious mind…she has a terrifying presence when angered…dispatches victims with little or no conscience…much the way any one would dispatch an insignificant insect. She started off her criminal career at a young age by removing small goods from the shops without the inconvenience of paying for them and later graduated to being a competent pick pocket and a semi professional forger." I suddenly realized that my fateful distraction from Winifred that day on the high street in Gravesend now had a name and a form.

Watching Sherlock eagerly rise from his seat as if to start the pursuit Mycroft stopped him by stating "I should tell you Sherlock that the two persons I have described are merely the people who were hired to abduct Miss Jeffery and deliver her to London for questioning. It is the people that hired them that we have to worry about."

Not sure where this was going I asked "What do we (meaning Sherlock and I) do next?" Mycroft never having dealt with these matters as his brother had looked to Sherlock for direction. Smiling assuredly, Sherlock stood up gestured toward me and confidently stated "I believe Mrs. Watson has exhibited considerable detective skills in Gravesend while conducting a preliminary cause of death and would be most suited to find out more about Miss Taggart.

Chapter 40

I tried my best to maintain my composure as I calmly replied "what document do you mean?" The man then closed the distance between us so that he was standing uncomfortably next to me. Shaking his head and giving me a look that one might give to a difficult child he continued impatiently "Miss Jeffery my colleagues and I do not have the time or patience to play games.

We know some time ago that you and a small group of people had entered the damaged interior of the St. Peter and St. Paul church to assess the damage. We also know that one of your party entered the sacristy, found the document in question and removed it. By the process of elimination (of course I knew he meant the death of Stan and Charles) and a somewhat botched and fruitless examination of your home we believe it is you who has the list and thus the reason for your being here."

Realizing that I had been found out and afraid of the fateful consequences of the discovery I decided to hold on to the faint chance that my disappearance had been discovered by Mary and Mr. Holmes and a rescue might be at hand. I cautiously repeated "what document do you mean?" I was unsure of his reaction to my continued denial the distinguished looking man (who had not introduced himself) turned and left the room to presumably discuss with others the next course of action leaving me alone to wonder what was next.

The unexpected outcome of my abduction meant that an impromptu meeting was now taking place in the dusty and unused office. Although most of the conversation was muffled by the thick door I caught the occasional word indicating their confusion and lack of direction as to how they were to proceed in retrieving the Survivors list.

After what seemed an eternity the barely audible conversation ended and the door opened. I was greeted with "Miss Jeffery you have placed us in a very awkward position. Having conferred with my colleges' a number of options have been discussed as to how to precede. Due to your status as a mystery writer the first two suggestions have been dropped from the discussion for the time being. It has been decided that you remain our guest at a rooming house not too far from this location.

Each day you will be brought from your lodgings to this room and you will be asked for your co operation in returning the document you claim to have no knowledge of. But I should warn you, if after a certain amount of time has passed you still choose not to co-operate... well you are the mystery writer and you should know how this story will end."

Chapter 41

At this point in my narrative there were two paths to follow. It was decided that Sherlock would take up the trail of Thomas Prescott to see if he could lead us to where Winifred had been delivered. I in turn was to take up the trail of Ashley Taggart to see what she knew in connection with Winifred's disappearance.

To this end, Sherlock's elder brother provided us both with as much information on the two suspects as he could. It wasn't disclosed at that moment but some time later Sherlock revealed to me that Mycroft had expressed his doubts about my detective abilities. "Sherlock, merely being the wife of Dr. Watson is hardly qualification enough to pursue someone like Miss Taggart." I was proud to hear that Sherlock's response to this doubt was that although I was not as experienced as John given the opportunity, could soon be.

After leaving Mycroft's office and knowing that time was against us we formulated a plan of action. Each morning we would meet for breakfast at my hotel to calculate the likely locations (from Mycroft's information) as to where we both might find our quarry. We would also return for dinner to pool what we had learned and gauge our progress.

Chapter 42

East Street Market known locally as 'The Lane', or 'East Lane', is a busy street market in Walworth in South London. It is large and vibrant and is good for vegetables, material and household goods. East Street is in the London Borough of Southwark and is between Walworth Road on the western side and the Old Kent Road on the Eastern side.

The market runs down East Street from the junction with Walworth Road to Dawes Street. The main entrance to the market is from Walworth Road. There has been street trading in the Walworth area since the 16th Century, when farmers rested their livestock on Walworth Common before continuing to the city.

During the industrial revolution, stalls lined the whole of the Walworth Road, but the market has only been officially running since 1880. The market today sells clothing, jewellery, cosmetics, household products, confectionary, fruit, and vegetables and for some it is a wealth of pockets and hand bags waiting to be picked.

I entered the busy market from Walworth road not sure if I would even catch a glimpse of Miss Taggart in the constantly moving crowd of vendors and shoppers, much less apprehend and her force her to share what she knew of Winfred's whereabouts.

Trying to blend in and remain as inconspicuous as possible because I was sure she would remember my face from our encounter on the high street in Gravesend I feigned passing interest in all the goods around me all the time watching out for her.

I had been walking back and forth through the market for about an hour without any success and was starting to be noticed by some of the vendors for not making any purchases when I witnessed a young lady generally matching the description of Miss Taggart. It appeared she was on a collision course with an older gentleman who was finishing his transaction with a fruit vendor.

I arrived just as Miss Taggart was backing away with a childlike expression upon her young face. She was apologizing innocently saying "excuse me sir I didn't see you standing there." The man smiling kindly was about to dismiss the accidental collision hoping that Miss Taggart had not been hurt, when I came up from behind.

Placing my hand securely on the young ladies shoulders thus letting her know I knew what had just taken place I firmly announced "young lady you will return the gentleman's billfold." Up until this point, the three of us had just been part of the pedestrian traffic making its way through the market.

It was at this point that the passers by stopped to see what my order was all about. I could detect a shared sense of disbelief. The gentleman who found his billfold had been skilfully removed from an inner pocket without his knowledge and from the female pick pocket who thought she would never be caught practising her craft.

As Miss Taggart reluctantly returned the purloined item to its owner the older gentleman opened the billfold to make sure that all the contents were intact. Now recovering from his shock stated "we should call a constable and have this thief arrested." Fearing that I might lose my one lead as to where Winifred may be located I assured him that once I had questioned her on some matters I would place the pick pocket into the care of the local constable.

"Come with me" I said to her in what I hoped was a commanding tone of voice. While maintaining my control over her I briskly walked Miss Taggart through the busy market, trying not to attract unwanted attention. I was looking for a secluded part of the market where whatever information that might be exchanged would not be overheard. When I located a deserted brick lined alcove (in a move that surprised me as much as the young lady) I placed both hands firmly on her young shoulders moved her until her back was to the wall and demanded "Where have you taken Miss Jeffery?"

Chapter 43

For the next few days while Sherlock and I were searching for Winifred her day consisted of being escorted in the morning by two non communicative male companions from a run down rooming house. It was a short trip as it was located a few short blocks away from WH Matthews & Co Residential Conveyancing office. Upon her arrival she was shown to a room that had become quite familiar.

Each day although the form and direction of questioning might change (depending on the person asking) the focus of the interrogation remained the same. Then one day the line of examination surprisingly changed and suddenly there was an apparent interest in her books.

Winifred was shrewd enough to know that the people who were her "hosts" had no real interest in the literary work of a female mystery writer from Gravesend. Obviously they had grown tired of Winifred's obstinate "what document do you mean" answer and hoped to lower her guard by changing the subject and getting her to talk about her work.

Winfred picks up the story…

I left the rooming house that had become my residence for an unknown period of time. I don't know if it had been chosen for its close proximity to where my daily interviews were to occur or if it had been chosen to demoralize my spirit because of its run down state.

I was not going to let my captors know how frightened I was in my less than acceptable accommodations, nor was I was going to let them know who had the Survivors list.

As before I was lead through the deserted office to what I began to think of as my interrogation room. I sat down in the same chair as last time watched my silent escort leave and awaited one of my three now familiar interrogators to enter the room. There was a longer than usual wait punctuated by what I thought was a short conversation in the office outside between two people. Then the door opened and I was facing a man I had never seen before.

The first thing that struck me about him was his attire. He looked less like the others who in any other circumstance might be professional men or bankers. This man looked more like a clerk in the men's clothing department of a reputable shop. As he entered he smiled extended his right hand in greeting and as the distance between us decreased he welcomed me with "Miss Jeffery what a pleasure to meet you."

Being momentarily caught off guard and not knowing how to respond I automatically rose from where I had been seated and shook his hand. Sitting back down and regaining my composure I wanted to know more about this apparent change in tactics. Feeling as if I had regained myself I fixed my visitor a look and calmly asked "Mr.?" then waited. Curiously it was almost as if he was searching though some card index at the library locating a fictitious name to use there was a noticeable pause then "Hewitt."

Deftly deflecting the interest from himself back to me he started "But I didn't come to talk about myself. When I heard you were here to clear up the matter of a misplaced document I asked if I could talk to you only about your books." Looking at Mr. "Hewitt" now sitting comfortably across the table from me he didn't strike as the sort of person who would be interested in reading mysteries written by a woman much less knowing anything about a female writer from Gravesend. But I welcomed the change (no matter as to the motive) from what was becoming a hostile and threatening line of questioning.

I could tell that either Mr. "Hewitt" or the people who were employing him had done their research on me. His literary line of questioning focused on two of my favourite mysteries The Pathway of Lost Souls and The Unicorn and the Wasp."

Trying to maintain my guard and keep my enthusiasm for my work in check I gave an outline and a synopsis of both stories. Then I went on to describe the character of Emily Porter who was the amateur and somewhat reluctant detective in both stories. As I was talking I could tell that Mr. "Hewitt" was skilled at his craft and why he had been chosen. He did from time to time direct the conversation back to where had he been instructed.

But like seeing a bright warning flare going up into the night sky I kept bringing the conversation back to either the setting of the first story which had been set in Gravesend or to the setting of the second story which was a country house in Sussex, or to my heroine Emily.

I could sense that as the conversation continued the facade of literary interest that Mr. "Hewitt" was trying to maintain was starting to erode. Also, that there was a growing frustration in his questioning because he was not getting the results he had been sent to retrieve.

Almost as if to end the interview there was a knock at the door…Mr. "Hewitt" got up went and opened it slightly. There was another somewhat muffled conversation then he turned in my direction. "Miss Jeffery I have to leave now" he looked at me for a moment as if he wanted to say something. I could sense from the change in his expression that his words could be over heard "I would suggest that you co operate with these people and give them what they want. Patience is a virtue and they have little left."

Chapter 44

The East India docks are located on the Thames between Blackwall Reach and Bugsby's Reach. East India men traded between Blackwall and Calcutta or other Indian ports, laden with the merchandise of two civilizations. The docks were initially designed to handle large East India men (ships) of up to 1000 tons. The basin, import and export docks could berth up to 250 sailing ships at a time. However, as the 19th century progressed, steamships also began to use the docks. Although they could not accommodate the larger vessels that used the Royal Docks or Tilbury, the East India Docks were frequented by the smaller steamers of the Union Castle and other shipping lines throughout the late 19th century and well into the 20th century.

Many businesses saw the advantages of the new enclosed docks. The East India Dock Company (formed in 1803) was given permission to build another dock at Blackwall to serve the vast shipping needs of the East India Company. As with the London Docks, the area around the East India Docks attracted other business. Pepper warehouses and spice-grinding operations sprang up in the area. Pubs, and supply shops opened to cater for the dock workers and ships deckhands employed there.

There was one particular unassuming pub close to the docks that was favoured by the heavy toiling labourers, the Mermaid Inn. It was a small, dimly lit and an unadorned sort of tavern (with a history dating back to the buccaneers) where a man could go to sit and down a pint of ale, eat a hearty meal in peace and forget about the monotony and drudgery of his employment for a time.

Although there were not always names attached to faces of the regular patrons everybody frequenting the Mermaid knew and trusted the ones they were drinking and eating with.

While I was dealing with Miss Taggart in the market a stranger in somewhat unfamiliar garb was seen entering the pub. Most of the activity stopped as he made his way towards the counter presumably to order food and drink. On hearing the stranger's unfamiliar accent those who had chosen to ignore him up till now suddenly took an interest in this new and unfamiliar patron.

Very few in England had any knowledge about the United States of America much less how its citizens looked and sounded until now "My name is Jack Johnson from Chicago" realizing this meant little to the inn keeper the stranger in his east coast accent continued on a more familiar tact "I'm looking for a man called Thomas Malone" not getting any response the stranger pressed on "He's known as the badger."

Suspiciously the inn keeper eyed the stranger and replied "The badger has been around, if he should come by later why you would want to see him?" The American smiled and answered "Back home he has quite a reputation as what you English would call a pugilist. While I was in London I wanted to meet him and discuss his style of fighting."

"I'll let him know you stopped by, is there any way the badger can reach you?" The American thought for a minute then said "It might be easier if I stop by later. "I'm very interested in meeting him I think he might know some things I would find most illuminating."

Chapter 45

Winifred goes on to describe the events after her last interrogation or interview had taken place.

Shortly after Mr. "Hewitt" departed the two non talking male companions entered to escort me back to the somewhat run down rooming house.

Silently escorted though the front door I was led up the facing set of stairs. At the top we turned right and walked down a short hallway which was covered in a threadbare carpet then one of the companions produced a skeleton key from his pocket opened the door in front of me and waited until I entered the single room.

As soon as I crossed the threshold I heard the door solidly close behind me and the key being turned in the lock to indicate that until tomorrow morning this small space was now my entire world. I had come to know that the monotony I was facing would be interrupted by my daily visit and interrogation and three uninspired and plainly cooked meals. The colour of the sunlight shining through the painted over widows blocked my view of the street thus denying me any land marks. I could however sense by the light creeping in when my next meal was due to be served.

The sun had started to stream through my heavily curtained windows when I heard a sharp rap on the door to my room accompanied by the abrupt announcement "breakfast."

Finishing getting dressed I hurried to the door as I heard the key in the lock then watched as it was being opened. As with each meal the same unhappy looking women stood in the hall bearing a meal tray. Each time the almost reluctant serving of food routine never varied. The tray was passed to me with the announcement "I'll be back in thirty minutes to retrieve it finished or not."

When the door was again closed and locked I very quickly made my way to the single table and chair which along with the single bed made up the entire furnishings of my room to eat a somewhat hurried meal. The first few meals eaten in this prison like room had proven that thirty minutes did not give me enough time to wonder about the source and nature of the meal in front of me. Further what was not consumed in such a short span of time was returned uneaten on the serving tray to the same unhappy looking woman.

Thinking like yesterday I would shortly after breakfast be escorted to my interrogation room for an increasingly hostile and threatening questioning I was surprised and a little worried to see that the sunlight coming into my room was a little brighter (indicating to me a passage of time) and I had not yet been called upon.

Chapter 46

When I located a deserted brick lined alcove in a move that surprised me as much as the young lady, I placed both hands firmly on her young shoulders moved her until her back was to the wall and demanded "Where have you taken Miss Jeffery?"

Only the briefest look of guilt passed her young face while I waited for the answer I was convinced she had. Then like clouds being dispersed by a breeze to reveal a sunny day her demeanour changed to that of an innocent and she very coyly replied "I don't know who you are talking about."

John had taught me that the ones who profess the most innocence are usually the guiltiest. Knowing that Winfred's safety was contingent on getting the information I needed I pushed the young lady just a little harder to the wall hardened the tone of my voice a little and continued.

"Are you not the young lady who removed certain articles from Miss Jefferies handbag while you and the young man you were with and were attending the Gravesend spring fete?

Not waiting for an immediate reply I continued "are you also the young lady who distracted me on the high street in Gravesend long enough to separate me from Miss Jeffrey allowing her to be abducted by an accomplice?" Not satisfied that I had convinced her I continued "are you not the young lady who was spotted at the train station in the company of an older man and Miss Jeffery leaving the Gravesend train?"

Miss Taggart stared defiantly at me and started to push herself away from the wall. "If you so much as take another step I shall loudly call for a constable to come and have you arrested' I cautioned her. "If how ever you chose to cooperate and give me the information I require I shall let you walk away. I could see Miss Taggart considering my offer.

I was certain that sooner or later she realized that she would find herself in a similar circumstance and with her lifestyle it would only be a matter of time before she would find herself in gaol. After considering for a brief moment Miss Taggart shared everything she knew about Winifred's whereabouts and I couldn't wait to share this information with Sherlock and hurried away

Chapter 47

By 8 p.m. the Mermaid was bereft of patrons who had gone home to tenement flats or back to the docks to finish loading and unloading cargo ships. Others had gone to find other ways to ease the burdens of their labours.

It was at this time the American Jack Johnson from Chicago entered and saw Thomas "the badger" Prescott standing at the counter placing an order for a drink. Not wanting him to slip away he quickly closed the distance. With a boisterous voice he announced "Mr. Malone what a pleasure to meet you." Thomas, momentarily caught off guard looked surprised the American continued with the introduction "Jack Johnson from Chicago."

Thomas quickly seeing through the disguise realized who was standing in front of him sarcastically returned "a pleasure to meet you Mr. Johnson or should I say Mr. Holmes." The inn keeper realizing the true identity of the now supposed American replied "well I would have never guessed." Thomas now feeling more secure about the situation continued "I assume Mr. Holmes you have not come to discuss pugilistic or boxing styles with me as the inn keeper had informed me. Perhaps you are interested in that meddling woman writer." Sherlock always the gentleman, corrected Thomas's disrespect for Winfred with "Yes, Miss Jeffery."

"Of what possible interest could she be to you?" The badger asked not sure of the connection between a consulting detective and a mystery writer. Sherlock returned "She is the close friend of Mrs. Mary Watson. Miss Jefferies mystery writer's curiosity got the better of her when she took the Survivors list from the church. I'm sure that if she had known how events would have turned out she could have chosen not to remove it or replaced it shortly after examining it.

Obviously it had more importance to the people who drew it up in the first place than to Miss Jeffery. As to my first involvement it was Miss Jeffery who contacted Mrs. Watson upon seeing my brother's name on the list assuming he had been eliminated." With a trip to the London hospital I found out that he had only suffered a relatively minor wound to his arm."

Stopping for a second to collect his thoughts Sherlock continued "It was the bungled break and entry of Miss Jefferies home and the three murders...two which occurred in Gravesend and one in London that my interest continued to grow. It appeared someone was going to extraordinary lengths to retrieve it."

Thomas had to admit to a certain level of admiration for the man standing in front of him. "I'm impressed with your knowledge but you have no idea of the significance of the Survivors list holds. Before we proceed, is it possible that you Mr. Holmes might like to share your knowledge of the document?"

Sherlock flashed the briefest of smiles…"Mr. Prescott I do not have all the information at this time. I am however interested in the current location of Miss Jeffrey's….I am but one of two dead ends you have arrived at."

Hoping to discover where Winfred was being kept…Sherlock pressed on "Since she can be of no real value to you and to the people who employ you it would be in the best interests of all if she was released." The badger looked at Sherlock with an evil gleam in his eyes "not true Mr. Holmes, if she genuinely doesn't have real knowledge of the Survivors list she still has some value in terms of…how should I say this…leverage."

Sherlock flashing back three years to Paris and remembering the unfortunate death of another woman that he could not save addressed Thomas almost as if he would carry out the act himself "if I find out that Miss Jeffery has been harmed in any way the person responsible will be held accountable."

Thomas self assuredly replied "I am sure I will pity the person who attempts this Mr. Holmes. The badger critically assessed Sherlock head to toe for a moment then calmly stated "But I have matters to attend to"…and as something of a parting compliment…"one of your better if not totally convincing disguises Mr. Holmes…although personally I always thought your Dutch bricklayer disguise was far more convincing."

With that Thomas the badger Prescott made his exit from the Mermaid…as the door closed behind him Sherlock was almost convinced he heard a mans low voice (who thought he might be out of earshot) say almost sarcastically "I will give your regards to Miss Jeffery when I see her next."

That barely audible phrase set off a reaction in Sherlock's mind and he was out the door and in pursuit of a person he thought might have uttered it and apparently held little value for human life. Catching up and matching his pace to the badger Sherlock briskly tapped him on the shoulder to get his attention. The badger stopped and turned in Holmes direction…looking some what irritated at this unexpected interruption of his journey Thomas asked "Is there something you have forgotten Mr. Holmes?"

"No there is nothing I have forgotten…but rather something you said as you left the Mermaid that indicates to me you may know where Miss Jeffery is being kept." Thomas smiled knowingly at Sherlock "even if I did know Mr. Holmes you would have to agree that I would be a fool to give such valuable information up." The badger thinking he held the high ground continued "after all, if a man has in his hand the winning cards in a game with high stakes he would be a fool to reveal what he has too early."

Sherlock with some irritation in his voice replied "Mr. Malone your contemptible arrogance will force me to take drastic measures." "Drastic measures Mr. Holmes?" In the past that would have meant John drawing his army service revolver and taking aim to motivate the suspect Sherlock thought to him self.

"I'm afraid this time you are out matched Mr. Holmes. Do you know why they call me the badger? Badgers despite their size are by their confrontational nature, a nasty animal. They are aggressive, they show no fear, are single minded in their assault, do not retreat but press their attack and their sharp claws and teeth are employed for only one purpose. Mr. Holmes, I admire such an animal and try to emulate as many of its talents and skills as I can."

Sherlock noticed that the stance of the badger was starting to change. Being unaware of Thomas's style of fighting he would have to take a moment and observe in order to defend him self accurately.

Thomas still somewhat in a relaxed state sized up Sherlock planning where to strike the first effective blow. He had no intent to kill Sherlock but rather to disable the consulting detective long enough for Thomas to make a clean escape.

Hoping he was lulling Sherlock into an unguarded state the badger continued "from your reputation I assume you are well versed in several different styles of fighting or combat?" In a rare show of pride Sherlock answered back "I have travelled to several countries and when one presents a particularly interesting type or form I make a study of it to include in my arsenal of defence. I can then draw on this knowledge when I am dealing with dangerous persons thus precluding the need for a fire arm."

Then in a radical change of character the badger dropped his London, Margate Road accent and started addressing Sherlock in an accent that any linguist would easily identify as coming from Dramorra, Ireland.

The badger smiled knowing in his mind what was about to take place. "Are you familiar with the type of fighting I make a living at?" Sherlock regarded Thomas with some disdain and answered "Bare knuckle boxing or fighting. The only sport, if indeed if it could be called a sport, that attracts people such as yourself to participate."

"You may look down on what I do for a living Mr. Holmes but it is a sport that serves many purposes." Sherlock countered "Other than knocking a man senseless to the ground or killing him outright for the financial gain of others, I see no purpose to this "sport.""

"It serves another less known but useful function to my purpose." Sherlock's interest was momentarily piqued "from time to time when I am employed, there are troublesome people who want to know too much about what I am doing or why. My particular expertize in the sport of bare knuckles boxing assures that they will no longer be troublesome."

As Sherlock saw the badger clench his right fist and draw his arm back in preparation to strike him Thomas said with great conviction "and you Mr. Holmes are starting to be quite troubling." Not being able to anticipate the speed and direction of his opponent's first blow Sherlock felt the badger's right fist violently connect with his lower left jaw.

Momentarily caught off balance Sherlock felt the pain from the point of impact radiate up into his skull. Regaining his equilibrium he realized the dangerous strength he was facing and why so many of the badgers opponents never lived to see the end of a fight.

Now striking a boxer's defensive pose Sherlock watched the badger trying to anticipate where and when he would strike next. Thomas smiled at his opponent's predictable defence and derisively commented "ah the Marquis of Queensbury rules then Mr. Holmes." "That" the badger said cockily "is where I have the advantage over you in my form of fighting there are no rules."

For the next few minutes Sherlock due to the unpredictable fighting style of the badger was forced to take a defensive stand to the badger's offensive stand. Blocking and equally suffering as many of the hard and sharp blows to his body as he was forced to endure.

When the badger realized that his opponent had more stamina and would not easily be disposed of he found for the first time he had to halt his attack and catch his breath. Putting his hands on his knees to draw in more breath Thomas looking up and grudgingly commented to Sherlock. "Mr. Holmes, you are proving to be a most worthy opponent, certainly far more challenging than other men I have fought. However this fight must come to an end."

Sherlock also catching his breath reached into an inner pocket to retrieve a handkerchief. He used it to wipe away the blood that had started to flow from his right nostril. The flow of blood started after he had received a particularly brutal smashing blow obviously intended to break his nose.

Noting that the crimson flow had stopped...Sherlock replaced the now soiled handkerchief...fixed the badger a particularly cold stare and calmly asked "Mr. Prescott do you have any knowledge of the Japanese fighting art of Aikido?"

Still catching his breath the badger shook his head no...as Sherlock began to instruct Thomas   he placed his feet shoulder-width apart, with one slightly further back, allowing him to change foot positions as he needed. This also allowed him to move his weight back and forth to parry each attack. Sherlock kept his knees slightly bent at all times to allow both quick and unfettered foot movement.

Like a school master instructing a class room full of delinquent children Sherlock began; "The art of Aikido evolved from a variety of classical Japanese combative arts. Many forms and movements in Aikido stem from sword, knife, stick, spear, or archery movements. However, the majority of Aikido comes from an extremely effective open-hand fighting art called *Daito-ryu Aiki-jujutsu.*

The hand and arm movements in aikido are mainly spirals and circles. Choppy cuts and swings like in other martial arts are mostly used to attack. The circular motion allows your arms to move with momentum when pulling your opponent through his attack. Strength is achieved through the continuous movement, while the hands remain open to grab and hold."

When Sherlock had finished the instruction his pose and mindset were one and he was fully prepared to defend himself against any assault from the badger. Thomas very much less than impressed with this unknown style of fighting commented "I'm impressed, or should I say that I am not, that you have travelled to another country to learn a fighting style that has no practical use in this country.

Here results are measured by the number of times a man's fist can connect with another to get the results desired. But as I stated earlier Mr. Holmes, I have matters to attend to" then thinking that the contest was already over and that Sherlock was disposed of "concerning Miss Jeffery. So I suggest we finish this." The badger took up his bare knuckle fighting pose and set to strike another blow against Sherlock.

But now the contest had unexpectedly changed because each time the badger tried to land a blow against Sherlock his fist instead of connecting with flesh passed by its target and was dissipated into thin air. Like a sapling moving in a summer breeze Sherlock fluidly moved to the left or the right to avoid being hit when a particularly fast blow was coming towards him he easily deflected it with his left or right arm.

Realizing that with each passing moment spent defending himself against the badger was one less moment that Winfred might have to live…and now fully realizing the real threat that Thomas might present Sherlock wrestled with a difficult decision. He decided to bring this contest to an end. With the next blow from the badger coming towards him rather than fluidly deflecting it Sherlock grabbed hold of the hand with his own left, in one assured move pulled the badger towards him and with his right he made a tightly clenched fist and directed it towards the badger's trachea.

With this somewhat violent action there was the fracturing sound of small bones being broken in the throat followed by the wheezes of a man now desperately gasping for air. Suddenly no longer able to breathe there was a final look of surprise and shock on the badgers face as his life slipped away. With that, Sherlock released his Aikido grip on him and let his now dead opponent fall to the street.

Chapter 48

As I had done for several mornings I chose a table in the busy hotel dining room where Sherlock and I could breakfast and be assured that our conversation would not be overheard. Sherlock's morning arrival seemed to take longer than usual because of the news that I wanted to share with him as to where Winifred was being held captive.

It was when the waiter was refilling my cup with freshly brewed coffee I saw Sherlock appear at the entrance to the dining room asking the server where I was seated. Seeing me he quickly made his way to my table.

As he sat down I could tell that a great weight had been lifted form his shoulders. Dismissing the attending waiter after pouring his cup of coffee and casually adding cream and sugar to the cup he announced "Mr. Malone, one of Miss Jefferies captors will no longer be an impediment to us locating her."

I quickly filled him in on what Miss Taggart had revealed of Winifred's whereabouts. At that instant we both stopped our breakfast looked at each other for a brief time and then spurring into action. Sherlock raised his hand into the air announced "waiter!" to one who was passing and asked him to bring the bill for the meal.

With Sherlock collecting his coat I collected mine along with my handbag. We both quickly made our way to the entrance of the Lancaster Gate hotel. There as fortune would have it was a motor taxi with its engine idling waiting for a fare.

With Sherlock entering first then myself as I closed the passenger door I gave the driver our destination "WH Matthews and company 109 Old Street, Stepney" turning around and looking a little surprised at a woman giving a destination the driver nonetheless tipped his cap politely and answered "yes miss." Although he didn't say anything as the motor taxi pulled away I could tell Sherlock was as concerned about Winifred's precarious state as I was.

Chapter 49

The motor taxi made a final left turn onto Old street and pulled up in front of what appeared to be a disused business. The faded sign read WH Matthews & Co., 109 Old Street below the title of the business. The sign still indicated the services it had offered some time ago; Residential Conveyancing -Company Commercial, Business -Commercial Property.

Peering through the large dust covered front windows the condition of the unlit outer office more than convinced both Sherlock and I that it had been some time since this office had transacted any type of business and it was not the sort of location to keep a hostage.

Before formulating any type of rescue Sherlock inquired as to whether I had the right address. I assured him that I made clear to Miss Taggart when I was questioning her in the market, that should she provide the wrong information I would make her life most difficult and her pick pocket days would come to an end. I warned her that I would not rest and would employee as many people as possible to follow her every move. I am confident this is the correct address.

Uncertain of what we would discover we proceeded to the front entrance. While Sherlock reached into an inner pocket to retrieve his infamous lock picking tools (a skill John had never agree with) I tried the door knob, it turned and I gently pushed the door inwardly.

We were both sure that the protesting sound the rusted hinges were making would attract unwelcome attention but as the door opened all the way all we were only met with was a thick coating of dust and silence. We carefully walked past the unused chairs, desks and filing cabinets any sounds of our proceeding foot steps indicating our progress to the back of the office were muffled by the thick carpet of dust under our feet.

At the back of the unoccupied office was a plain wall and set in it was a door which at first sight Sherlock and I presumed was a rear exit to a back lane. To both Sherlock's and my surprise there was a band of warm electric light shining out from under the bottom of the door.

Quickly formulating a plan, Sherlock indicated that he would enter the lit room first (then I would follow) to deal with whoever might be occupying the room. With a decisive turn of the door knob and his shoulder to the door to force it open should it be locked the door burst open to reveal quite a different sight from the room we had just left.

The clean moderately sized room was lit from electric light fixtures mounted on the two dark oak panelled side walls. Occupying most of the space was a long oblong table surrounding by matching chairs. At the head of the table much to our surprise sat a gentleman who apparently had been unmoved by our arrival.

Closing the file he had been studying he calmly looked up at us both and said "ah Mr Holmes and Mrs Watson. It is a pleasure to meet the great detective and the widow of his famous biographer. I had no doubt that with your combined skills you would arrive here to locate Miss Jeffery. As you can see, she is not here." "I must comment on your friend Mrs Watson. She has certainly proven to be persistent in denying any knowledge of the Survivors list or of its contents.

Less civilized individuals would have resorted to more persuasive methods to obtain the information but that was not our intent. So while Miss Jeffery can not serve her primary function of returning the list, she still has some value as leverage against those (here he stopped and gave both Sherlock and myself a hard look) who might know of its whereabouts."

Sherlock growing tired of this line of conversation and the superior attitude of the man sitting at the table interrupted "and where is Miss Jeffery at this moment? "For our purposes Mr Holmes she is safe. But with your unannounced visit she will have to be moved." Fearing for her life I burst out "I want Winfred returned now!" The man gave me a particularly condescending smile and coldly asked "and what can you, Mrs Watson do to make that happen?"

Chapter 50

During my final days visiting with John at St. Bartholomew's hospital he and I tried to share as much with each other as we could knowing that our time together was growing short. We relived the events of our first meeting; our marriage, shared memories of the home we had built together, the many memories in it we had created, our summer vacations together, Christmases, the trying times during the war, John's role as Sherlock's chronicler, our shared personal friendship with the consulting detective and of course my husbands last request to document further Sherlock Holmes cases.

The most difficult request was saved for last. I could tell that my husband had been struggling with asking me for some time but knew what he wanted to discuss. John felt that what he was proposing might some day be necessary. That day was now. I reached into my hand bag withdrew John's service revolver pointed it at my tormenter and again requested Winfred's release.

Sherlock was both impressed and a little surprised at my unexpected solution to what was amounting to an impossible impasse. The man at the table was having a less than favourable reaction at seeing a woman drawing a weapon from her handbag obviously having been trained as to how to use it and now it was aimed at him.

Rendered speechless and feeling the colour drain from his face he weighed his options at that moment and shakily returned "I will take you to her immediately."

Winfred's place of confinement was not far from the abandoned office. It was typical of a lot of the rooming houses located in Stepney. It was a two story structure with faded paint, ramshackle in appearance and much in need of repair. We carefully entered the rooming house then the man said he would have to locate the lady who held the key to Winfred's room.

As Sherlock and the man set off into the interior of the rooming house to locate the house keeper I surveyed the surroundings and thought that we couldn't release Winfred soon enough. While I was taking stock of the scene from somewhere near the rear of the house I heard a woman's name being called in a somewhat nervous manner, then a woman's impatient voice replying back "I'm coming I'm coming."

Returning with her escort to the entrance the house keeper eyed me suspiciously and "you know I can't release the lady without proper instructions." Sherlock with a new found pride in me returned with a nod in my direction "I think you will find instruction enough in Mrs. Watson's pistol."

With that, the four of us proceeded up a flight of rickety stairs to the second floor and then found ourselves facing a locked door. The housekeeper slowly inserted the key into the lock and turned it.

Sherlock reached over and turned the door knob. The door opened inwardly to reveal a very surprised and very much relieved Winfred Jeffery. Coming toward the door of her very bare room Winfred exclaimed "Mary, Mr. Holmes, it is good to see you both again."

Epilogue

There are three final parts of this chronicle to document. The first being that after rescuing Winfred and having her agree to stay at the Lancaster Gate hotel until she was recovered enough to return to Gravesend, Sherlock went to see his brother to close the matter of the Survivors list.

It was agreed between Sherlock and his brother that due to the political sensitivity of the document it would be placed in a safety deposit box at a bank somewhere in the United Kingdom and that only Mycroft would have any knowledge of its location.

A few days later Winfred decided she was well enough to make the journey to her home. "My home and my writing are both in shambles and I should return to tend to both." She explained to me as she was finishing her packing. Later with a motor taxi ride from the hotel all we arrived at the train station to see Winifred off.

As we were walking together through the busy and bustling station to the platform Sherlock excused himself to allow Winfred and I time alone. "I will say my goodbye now Miss Jeffery and I wish you well on whatever new book you have set your mind to write." "Mary I will see you later for dinner." Tipping his hat to Winfred, Sherlock made his way back to the street entrance.

"Will I see you again?' Winfred asked as we got to our destination and waited for the conductor to announce "all aboard." I smiled and answered "I'm going to stay in London and spend some time with Sherlock. I haven't seen him in over three years and there is much to talk about.

I am sure he has plans to return to Doncaster soon and when he does I will come back to Gravesend. Besides, there is the re dedication of St. Peter and St. Paul church to attend. With that Winifred boarded her train with a final wave from the train's window began her journey home. That left me with only one final goodbye to attend too.

My final time with Sherlock was as much about what was said as what wasn't. We talked about the things that had happened to Winifred. With the promise that if I documented the affair I was not to romanticize it as he claimed John had done.

Sherlock commended me on my new found skills as a detective and my ability to adapt to difficult situations. Even though he never expressed the words I felt that at least for a short time I had stepped into John's shoes and that Sherlock was grateful that I had.

"And what is next for you Mary?" Sherlock asked as we were having dinner later that evening at the hotel. I answered I would stay on for a little while longer, see to the house, then return to Gravesend to keep Winfred company and encourage her to start writing again

"And what is next for you Sherlock?" I asked in return. He replied "I think a much needed vacation to the South of France in particular Avignon in the Provence Alps Cote d'Azur region. I have heard of the restaurant called l'Orangerie located there. It is a small eatery located at the Place Jerusalem, just a few minutes walk from the Place de l'Horloge."

Sherlock let out an unexpected sigh with his final comment concerning our conversation "I think my bees will survive the lack of my companionship while I take in the French sun and cuisine."

Early the next morning I accompanied Sherlock from the hotel to the station to see him off on the train that would take him to Dover then across the channel to France. There was little conversation between us during the ride. As we then walked through the busy and hectic Paddington train station concourse I tried to think of things to talk about to delay his departure.

Then I remembered "Sherlock. I happened to glance at a newspaper this morning and saw that Miss Taggart had been arrested. Apparently she made the mistake of pick pocketing an off duty police constable and now she is awaiting trial." "I had a feeling Mary" Sherlock sagely returned "that with such persons as her, justice may be cheated for a time but eventually served."

Finally arriving where he would shortly board his train I suddenly thought about Christmas. "Sherlock" I started while recalling the last Christmas we had all spent together "I was thinking of inviting a few friends to spend the festive season at my home.

The house has seen too many quiet Christmases' it would be nice to hear the sound of festive conversation and laughter again and I would like it if one of those voices was yours"

Sherlock gave me a smile I had only seen one time before, took my hands gently in his and said "yes." Before we knew it the Dover train had pulled into the station and was in front of us when we both heard the conductor telling all the passengers to board. With all that had been said and shared the only thing left was to exchange simple "goodbyes."

I sadly watched Sherlock board the carriage, and then he unexpectedly stopped before entering turned and looked kindly at me. As he smiled one more time at me the conductor said to him "the train is leaving the station you had better take your seat sir" before following the instruction Sherlock raising his right hand in a salute said directly to me in a warm and enthusiastic voice "Well done Watson! Without any hesitation I replied back "Well done Holmes!"

The End

Sherlock Holmes and The Mystery Writer notes:

As Mary Watson stated at the beginning of this record *"Please note…to any long time devoted follower familiar with what has been referred to or known as the "Sherlock Holmes Canon" the following narrative may seem some what unfamiliar (as in being written by a woman) you will no doubt miss seeing and reading such familiar terms my husband used through out his writing such as "Holmes" and "my friend" in the text of my account when specifically referring to Sherlock."*

When I started to write this story I felt as if the canon or formula for writing another Sherlock Holmes story had been exhausted. And rather than write a story that would not even vaguely resemble anything that Sir Arthur Conan Doyle may have written, I decided to follow a different path.

Having brought Mary Watson out of the shadows so to speak in my last story and making her a real person and part of the story I started to wonder if she had learned enough from John to take over his role with Sherlock…to my surprise as the story went along Mary Watson rose to the challenge…so much so that in the end she receives rare praise and a formal acknowledgment from Sherlock.

To make a simple switch from him to her by having John just retire would not be unbelievable and would challenge the whole purpose of the story. It was John's service as a medical doctor during the Afghan war…and either suffering some old war wound or illness he contracted allowed me to write the hospital scene where he hands his dying request to Mary to continue chronicling.

I took a lot of criticism for "killing off" John Watson. Surprisingly enough from people who have read Sherlock Holmes stories as well from people who only know about the great detective and his chronicler by reputation. However I think I redeemed myself and made peace with both groups in how I ended this story.

On the matter of "killing off" where after a long fight to the death Sherlock finally dispatches Thomas "the badger" with a fatal blow to the throat…to avoid just trailing off I finish that part of the chapter with only the badger's death. I am sure as any good citizen Sherlock would bring this matter to the attention of the police. Although as to how he would explain the death with out implicating himself would be interesting.

I should give you a word of caution before going down a strange and unfamiliar path (as I have chosen writing an original Sherlock Holmes story). When writing the first two, they came more or less preassembled, as pastiche stories (as they are known). Where the writer takes parts from different Sherlock Holmes stories combines them, and then writes a narrative to bind them all together. The third because it is an original took a lot more thought and effort and much longer to write compared to the first two

Outside of Sherlock Holmes, his brother Mycroft, John and Mary Watson all of the characters in the story are either original or are based on real people, friends and family.

The story is loosely founded on the conspiracy surrounding the sinking of the Lusitania (thus bringing the United States into the First World War and the people who may have been involved in it (thus the Survivors List) as well as the political unrest that was taking place in Ireland at the time.

One final note, as for this writer there will be one last mystery where Sherlock Holmes and Mary Watson collaborate together on a case. After that Mr. Holmes will slip into detective history and the widow of a dear friend will take up the detective reins.

Fred

Dedications

My many thanks to all the following people for making this book possible.

To:

Dianne... my editor, whose great work made my last book and this one a best seller

Audrey... for suggesting the location of the story, Gravesend

Ashley... for inspiring the character of Ashley Laurinda Taggart

Thomas...for inspiring the character of Thomas Malone Prescott

Andy... for inspiring the character of Andrew Foster Perry

Lynne ... for inspiring the character of Madam Liliya Cosmina Jarkovácz

A special thanks to Agatha Christie for inspiring the character of Winifred Elizabeth Margaret Jeffrey

To the staff of Williams Fresh Café locations here in Brantford.

Thanks for making available a great place to write…along with providing delicious food and excellent coffee.

Research references for Sherlock Holmes and The Mystery Writer

Agatha Christie – The Woman and Her Mysteries – Gillian Gill

The Life and Crimes of Agatha Christie – A Biographical Companion to the works of Agatha Christie – Charles Osborne

Agatha Christie – An Autobiography - William Collins and Sons - London

The Greatest Lies in History – Spin double speak; buck passing and official cover ups that shaped the world. - Part 2 – Pointing the way to Pearl Harbour - Alexander Canduci

Save Undershaw

The author and publisher support the campaign to save and restore Sir Arthur Conan Doyle's former home. Undershaw is where he brought Sherlock Holmes back to life, and should be preserved for future generations of Holmes fans.

Save Undershaw www.saveundershaw.com

Facebook www.facebook.com/saveundershaw

You can read more about Sir Arthur Conan Doyle and Undershaw in Alistair Duncan's book (share of royalties to the Undershaw Preservation Trust) – An Entirely New Country and in the amazing compilation Sherlock's Home – The Empty House (all royalties to the Trust).

Also from MX Publishing

From one of the world's largest Sherlock Holmes publishers, dozens of new books novels from top Holmes authors.

Visit the Sherlock Holmes Books page on Facebook for the latest releases:

www.facebook.com/BooksSherlockHolmes